…but Esau I Hated

By Stuart Thaman

…But Esau I Hated

Nef House Publishing

First Edition: January 2013

Cover Art by Will Olthouse
www.unsilentwill.com

ISBN-10: 0615746691

Prologue

His fist punched straight through the cheap plaster wall. It left a clean, almost perfectly cylindrical hole in the white wall of the tiny basement. Grabbing the edge of the nearest wooden stud with his strong hand and using his other arm, his human arm, to tear away at the plaster, he began to rip chunks out of the wall. He could see the lights now, blue and red, and that awful spotlight shining through the tiny window at the top of the wall to his left. He knew they were close, closer than they had ever been before. His arm worked furiously at the wall, tearing giant chunks of plaster away with every clawing swing.

He looked like he might only be eighteen years old, but the dirt in his brown hair and the torn up clothes he wore gave him the rugged air of someone twice his age. The determination in his eyes was nothing short of terrifying.

Blood was starting to trickle down his arm from the missing fingernails on his left hand. He gritted his teeth and pulled more plaster away as the light from the window, now accompanied by the hurried footsteps of leather boots, shone brighter and glinted off of a metallic object behind the edge of the plaster. The look of fierce determination on his face was momentarily replaced by a slight smile as his hand grasped the metal and began to twist the handle.

He heard the battering ram shatter the door to the house. "Idiots, the door wasn't even locked, you could have just walked in." Knowing that he was out of time, he gave a primal growl and put his shoulder into the wall, clearing out the rest of the plaster and sending a cloud of dust and splinters into his eyes. He grasped the metal handle with both hands and pulled for all his might, knowing that his time was at an end. The boots on the staircase behind him confirmed his fears.

"Stop! Freeze! Hands in the air!" He heard the shouts, the screams of the officers behind him. The bright white beams of their flashlights illuminated the safe in front of him, the reflection from the metal combined with the dust in his eyes almost blinding him. He tightened his grip on the latch and pulled again, electrical signals travelling down the synthetic nerves from his brain and into the arm, telling it to use every last reserve of power, knowing that if he could just open the safe, everything would be fine. He would live through this night. He would live through tomorrow. His gut churned and he almost burst into tears when he saw the dial on the side of the safe.

The combination! How could he forget the combination? Without entering the proper sequence into the dial, he would never open the safe. His hands slowly fell to his sides, defeated, his head hanging low. He knew he was beaten. The combination was somewhere in his head, to be sure, he just didn't have the time to remember it. The police already had him surrounded. His days of running were finally finished, this time for good. He dropped to his knees and started to bring his hands up to the back of his head, a final gesture of submission, when he heard the distinct sound of a steel baton being extended.

The dirty and sweaty teenager closed his eyes and grimaced, expecting the brains to be bludgeoned from the back of his skull when he heard a second sound, one he knew well. It was the sound of a revolver being drawn from an old leather holster. The Major had come as well. Without turning around he knew exactly what the scene behind him looked like. Six, maybe ten, armed response officers stood behind him in their black armor, weapons drawn, all trained on his back, their little red lasers moving in tight circles on his jacket. At least one of them had a baton out, he knew that with certainty.

What he now knew to be a fact, and the most daunting fact of the entire situation, was that the Major was standing in the middle of the group, probably wearing something incredibly fancy and entirely inappropriate for police work, that was the Major's style. He could see the Major standing there behind him, smug expression on his face, that ancient pearl-handled revolver in his gloved hand.

"My goodness boys! What do we have here? It looks like this little chase is finally at its end. And my, how I was beginning to relish it all! Truly son, I do enjoy a good chase." It was the Major without a doubt. That slow, incredibly thick western accent was unmistakable. The Major always had a way of speaking that convinced everyone in the room that he had recently kicked in a saloon door in the old west. No one knew if the Major honestly believed himself to be the sheriff of an old town in the Wild West or if he just enjoyed his childhood fantasy of cowboys and Indians so much that he never stopped playing. Whatever the case may be, the Major was a sadistic, relentless, psychopath with a massive ego and an ironically small stature.

"I'm sorry Major, I didn't rob no stagecoach and I never started no brawl in the tavern, I swear it!" He chuckled as he said it, doing his best to mock the Major with his horrible imitation of the old west. The barrel of the Major's revolver was cold, unusually cold against his neck. The boy was sweating from his ordeal with the plaster wall and swore he could feel the beads of sweat starting to freeze against his neck. It sent shivers down his spine and made his entire body tingle.

Suddenly, as quickly as his neck had gone cold, it was hot and sweaty again, the barrel removed. He could hear the Major take a few hesitant steps back. He heard the clicking noise as the hammer of the old revolver was pulled back and the chamber rotated to line a bullet up with the firing mechanism. "No!" the kneeling kid screamed, "you can't just shoot me! You have t-"

The sound of the gunshot surprised him more than anything. He honestly just thought this was another mind game, another way for the Major to take control, to intimidate him. Pain didn't even register, everything happened so fast. Why had the Major shot? Did the law not require him to be arrested? All of those threats that the Major always made, saying he would kill him if he ever caught him, those were more than just empty words?

No, he couldn't die like this. He hadn't gotten back to her, he hadn't found her, hadn't saved her. He knew he was crying as he tumbled forward into the hole he had made in the wall. The tears weren't because of the pain; he hadn't even felt that yet. The tears flooded his face as he thought of her, how he had failed her. How he would never see her again. Well, maybe if he didn't die he would be fortunate enough to be taken to the same place they had taken her and then he would finally know what happened to her, he thought to himself. It was little consolation.

He heard the shouts of confusion ringing out behind him, the chatter on the radios, the commands issued in harsh tones. He heard them, but could not comprehend. The floor beneath him seemed oddly comforting and familiar, cool against his sweaty cheek. His vision was blurry with red - his hands must be covering his crying face, his bloody hands. Thoughts of her rushed through his mind as he felt the blood welling up in his mouth and knew that one of his lungs must be punctured. He barely even noticed the small bullet hole in the wooden stud right in front of his chest.

Thick blood started to dribble out of his mouth feebly as his vision went completely black, his hands still clutching at his face. Above the din of chaos behind his slumped form, all he could hear was the distinct sound of the Major laughing. That infuriating forced accent and the sobs of uncontrollable laughter were the last things he heard before he plummeted into a world of dark oblivion.

Chapter 1

A harsh knock on the door woke the Major from his daydream and brought him back to reality. "Come in, come in" he called out in his trademark western accent. He closed the book in front of him and returned it to the top drawer of his new oak desk. The Major's gloved hand locked the drawer with a tiny brass key he wore on a chain around his neck, next to a pair of old, bloodstained and dented dog tags.

A new recruit stiffly opened the door and took a step inside the office before offering a rigid salute. "Yeah, what is it son?" He growled at the new policeman. The Major hated new officers. So full of pride, so smug and crisp, never to be found at fault for anything, they annoyed him. He hadn't bothered to learn any of the new officers' names in at least five years. He relished the fear he saw so plainly on this recruit's cleanly shaven face.

"Captain McCreary requests you in his office, sir" the young man awkwardly shouted, still holding the salute.

"Tell him I'll come see him when I'm finished with all of this paperwork." The Major didn't even bother to look the man in the eye as went back to the massive stack of papers on his desk.

"Captain said you are to come at once. He told me to escort you to his office myself, said it was urgent, sir." Fear was the only emotion accompanying the man's quavering words.

"Oh all right!" the Major shouted, frustrated. "I'll be up in a minute, and I'll not be dragging some homesick puppy dog of an officer all the way to McCreary's office! Get out of here." The recruit didn't budge from his stance just inside the door. The Major slowly got to his feet and grabbed his faded leather hat from its hook by the window and made for the door. The nervous recruit followed him all the way to the elevator at the end of the hallway.

"I can handle it from here, Officer…." The Major let his voice trail off, thinking that if perhaps he used a bit of kindness, he would get the man to leave.

"Sandusky, sir. Officer Sandusky. I just started last week. I've been looking forward to finally meeting you." The Major used one strong hand to keep the smiling new recruit from joining him in the elevator. As the doors closed, he shouted to the poor man that he would tell McCreary that he did his job well and delivered the message.

"It has been quite a long time since I have come all the way up to the 17th floor, Bill. Must be terribly important to send a halfwit recruit to fetch me. Do you remember the days when I used to sit behind that enormous desk and order you to come see me?" The Major shook his head, looking at his boss as he sat in one of the plush leather chairs. "Well, back in my day, I always went to my subordinates personally whenever there was an issue. I never sent a patsy to deliver my messages. Oh, how times have changed." The Major said it all with a smile on his face as he gazed out the window at the city he was sworn to protect. He put his feet up comfortably on McCreary's desk and sighed, wondering what this was all about.

"I don't remember asking you to sit, Major." Captain McCreary said the words with more anger than he wanted. The Major took his feet off the desk and sat up straight but made no effort to rise from the chair. "Fine, be like that. But tell me now, why on Earth did you shoot him? Why did you have to shoot the poor kid? Everything you did, apart from being illegal, was highly unethical and beneath you. I wouldn't have picked you for one to let his emotions cloud his judgment. Now I have the Mayor to answer to, the press all over the parking lot, hell, I've had to quarantine the entire response unit until I can get this mess straightened out. You've really gone off the deep end this time Major. If you weren't so good at your job and such an old friend, I would have you suspended and thrown in jail for all this!" The captain slammed his fist down on the desk to accentuate his point.

To be honest, it had been a blind moment of rage. The Major never intended on killing the poor kid, at least not right away. He needed to interrogate him, to get answers. How had the poor little bastard survived in the first place? When the Major's finger had pulled the trigger, sending a bullet into the kid, the Major had been just as surprised as everyone in the room. It wasn't part of the plan, shooting him in cold blood like that. Of course, the Major reminded himself, as long as the kid was dead, it didn't matter. It wouldn't hurt his mission to not have the only survivor interrogated, it would just be a nuisance. Shooting and killing the kid would have eventually happened anyways.

The Major said nothing. In his mind, everything had been a success. He had finally finished his last case. He could retire now, maybe move to the country and raise horses like he always dreamed about. "What's your point, Bill?"

"Lucky for you, the kid lived. He's banged up, lost a lung, tore three fingernails off his hand, and dislocated his wrist. Now I just have to play this off like some sort of accident, or temporary moment of rage, instead of having an internal investigation for murder on my hands."

The words hit the Major as visibly as if he had just been stabbed in the back. He lived! That *did* change things. How had the kid survived? It was a pistol shot, point blank to the back, he should have died in that dingy basement. The knuckles on his hands went white and he thought he might shatter the wooden chair in his disbelief.

"Where is he?" The Major almost screamed the words, his rage playing out in full.

"Come on Major, you actually wanted the poor kid to die?" The blood was visibly boiling beneath the Major's skin, his face turning dark red as he gripped the chair. "You know what? You *are* getting that suspension. You need to take some serious time off to think about your life and get your head back on right. Two weeks, Major. Go home, get some sleep, buy an expensive bottle of whatever it is you like to drink, hell, go to a bar and talk to a woman! It's been what, 6 years? Sheila isn't coming back. You need to figure out where your life is and what you're doing everyday when you come to work."

"Where is he?" he growled again, spit flying from his mouth. The Major had injected a small satellite transmitter into the neck of the kid, wanting to be sure that the survivor never left his grasp again. If the boy lived through the gunshot wound, the hospital would have surely done x-rays, surely frying the transmitter, making it useless. The realization only added to the Major's mounting anger. If he couldn't get Captain McCreary to tell him where the kid was being held, he might lose him for good.

"You honestly think I'm going to tell you where this kid is being treated when you act like some sort of rabid animal in my office? Go home, Major. I'll see you back in the office in two weeks. This whole situation better be cleared up in your head by then."

McCreary had a soft heart and the Major knew it. The Major had been able to play McCreary for years - all it took was hitting a couple sensitive buttons. "No, you're right Bill. I've lost my touch. Ever since Sheila left me, I haven't been the same, you know that. You know that better than anyone." He hung his head low, playing the remorseful part perfectly.

"I won't try to find the kid. I just want to send him a card, some chocolate, or whatever it is that kids like these days. You know, the same sort of stuff I sent your son before he died, an apology of sorts. I understand though, I wouldn't tell a psychopath gun cop like myself where he was either. I've got some money saved up, I'm going on vacation. Don't bother trying to get in touch while I'm gone, I'll hopefully be drunk the entire trip, stumbling down some street, wondering where my hotel is." The Major even managed a laugh to make it all seem genuine.

"See you in two weeks, Bill." All traces of the Major's old west accent were replaced by a sad tone of defeat and misery. The Major stood up and shook McCreary's hand before turning for the door.

"Major" McCreary called after him. "I'm sorry it has to be this way. Thanks for taking it like a man. No, like a friend. I don't even know why I'm telling you this. The kid, whatever his name is, is being treated downtown. Saint Hubert of Liege Hospital, across from the train station, you know it. Don't go near him, mail him something if you must, but don't speak to him, Major. I have him under twenty four hour surveillance. There is an officer outside his room day and night who won't let you in. I've also got him handcuffed to the bed; he *is* under arrest you know. This will all be over by the time you get back."

"Thanks Bill. It means a lot. I'm sorry I got carried away. It won't happen again." The Major had him. He always knew how to get exactly what he wanted from his soft-hearted boss. It was almost too easy.

"Oh, Major!" McCreary shouted down the hallway at him, "doctors said he had some kind of burn on the back of his neck, they think it was liquid nitrogen, I suppose you don't know anything about that, right?"

"Schnapps."

"What does that have to do with a burn on a kid's neck? Are you trying to tell me that schnapps did it?"

"You were wondering what I drink, I like to drink schnapps. Usually peppermint or cinnamon flavored. My grandfather always drank schnapps so I guess I learned to like it from an early age and never stopped. See you in two weeks, Bill. Don't let this place go to hell while I'm gone!" Checkmate. The Major had won and he knew it. His smile lasted all the way down the elevator to his office, as he got into his car, and only grew when he took out the massive bottle of recently purchased peppermint schnapps from a brown paper bag. The Major threw himself upon the only couch in his small apartment, reaching for the locator that was meant to track the small device now inserted in the kid's neck. It was blank, just like the Major had assumed. "Doesn't matter now anyways," he grumbled to himself, thinking of how easy it had been to play the old police captain, "I have everything I need."

The Major would take some of McCreary's advice, at least. He knew exactly where the kid was, and he knew he would be there for a very long time. He kicked his boots off, took off his old leather hat, clicked on the television, and resigned himself to the bottle. With two full weeks to take care of everything before McCreary found out what was going on, the Major figured that he had a few nights to waste at the bottom of a glass bottle. A few nights of getting drunk wouldn't hurt. The Major fell asleep with a smile on his face, an empty bottle in his hands, and Sheila on his mind. Checkmate.

Chapter 2

He woke up slowly, in more than just a tired fog. He could feel the drugs in his system, slowing his thoughts, slowing his senses, slowing everything. As his eyes gradually opened and he began to recognize his surroundings, his first thought was on the intravenous line dangling above him, connected to the needle in his arm. The kid strained his newly awakened senses to read the label on the pouch of clear liquid slowly dripping into his body but was forced to fall back.

"Not going to wake up today, are you? Well, I wouldn't even want to if I were you. Those government boys have been here all week, keep talking about reinstating the death penalty, just for you." It was an older woman's voice, probably a nun or a nurse. "The doctors won't let them tell the public though, probably for your own good. I couldn't imagine the riots we would see if every Catholic in America knew the kid who blew up the Vatican was in this hospital. Yeah, stay sleeping, probably for the best."

The nurse continued to move about the room, checking instruments, casually whistling to herself as she went about her work, utterly oblivious to the now very conscious patient lying in the bed, listening to her every movement, memorizing every last word.

Why did the nurse say the Vatican 'blew up'? That's news to me. So, the death penalty. It really isn't surprising. I mean, it was Easter Sunday and everyone in the Vatican just fell over, dead. All of them. They all just died. Everyone except for me. I was there, to be sure, but nowhere near the epicenter. That's how I remember it, at least. One minute I was having a great time with my friends, the next minute, everyone was dead.

Everything started to rush back and it all replayed in my mind as though it was happening again.

I was relaxing on a nice Sunday morning with my four best friends when it all happened. The five of us were all in the jacuzzi on our hotel veranda. We had just ordered room service when Joel dropped the cap off of his strange bottle of Italian water we all made fun of him for drinking. "I am just more cultured than you filthy peasants." He always said that when he drank the Italian water. "When I visit a country, I like to become one of the locals, not just a mere tourist." Everyone hated him for being such a snob, and beyond that, the water was terrible. Joel dropped the cap into the bubbling water as Owen punched him in the arm, teasing him again about his disgusting Italian bottled water. I curled my body up as I dove my head into the scalding water to grab the bottle cap before it got lodged in a vent or drain and broke the entire jacuzzi.

      Then it happened. It was like a subtle vibration at first, surprising, but not alarming. Like a few heavy trucks had just passed underneath our balcony, except there was no noise. No sound ever accompanied the vibration. Then it got more intense. I grabbed the bottle cap in my palm and tilted my head to look up at my friends for some explanation. Everything shifted suddenly, as if a giant translucent wave had hit the whole hotel. My entire field of vision jolted forward slightly, and then backward, then settled back to normal as the vibration died down. Still frozen underwater, I believed it to simply be a trick of the light. Then a drop of blood hit the surface of the water and I knew something was wrong.

My four friends in the jacuzzi with me slumped down into the water. Their mouths were open, their eyes rolled back, they were clearly dead. One of them was bleeding, I'm not sure where from. The jacuzzi jets were turning the water into a maelstrom of blood. I didn't know what would happen if I rose out of the water. I held my breath, surrounded by my dead friends, for what seemed like hours. Their bodies just floated there, half submerged in the bubbles of the jets, bumping into each other and occasionally bumping into me.

My lungs began to burn and I glimpsed the bottle of Italian water being tossed around above my head. I reached my arm, my metal prosthetic arm, above the water and grabbed the bottle. Pouring its remaining contents into the water I brought the bottle down fast to my lips, hoping to breathe what air I could from the bottle.

It didn't work. Of course it didn't work! It was a stupid idea. If, as I believed, something had happened to the air above the water, what good would bringing it down bottled do? It was now or never. I steeled what was left of my nerves and burst out of the water, looking around frantically and gasping for air. Nothing seemed to move. My friends, the only other people in the hotel room, were all floating haphazardly around my legs, their blood and hair coating my shins. The air was still, everything was silent. No birds chirped or sang, nothing. A few cars rolled into each other idly on the street below the balcony, grinding and scraping. Everything was just dead, except for me.

I stepped out of the hot churning water and moved into the room to grab my clothes and dry off. I kept looking at my friends, all slumped over in the jacuzzi, all dead. The tops of their heads kept hitting each other as I got dressed, my eyes never leaving the gruesome scene. I couldn't just leave them like that.

I spent a couple hours dragging their lifeless bodies out of the jacuzzi and into the room, constantly having to stop and look away to keep myself from heaving. I didn't know where to put them. I had nowhere to bury the corpses and I couldn't just let them float in the hot water of the jacuzzi. Seeing them all lined up, side by side, on the hotel room floor made me sick. I vomited into the trash can until my gut hurt too badly to throw up again. I kept glancing back at my friends after every retch. It only kept making me vomit more.

I decided that the best I could do was make them look peaceful. I put two bodies in each of the king sized beds in the suite and then gathered my belongings. Looting the belongings of my four closest friends made me twinge with guilt more than once, but they were dead, I reminded myself, they didn't need material possessions anymore. I told myself over and over again that they would want me to take what they had and try to survive.

With one last look at the solemn resting place of my roommates, I opened the door and peered out into the hotel hallway. A few paces down the hall was the room service cart. The server was slumped in a heap on the floor next to the covered cart, a small line of blood trickling down his chin and staining his blue uniform. I silently crept down the hall until I was right next to the cart and listened for the server's breathing. I knew he was dead before I even started walking towards him but I had to be sure. The entire hallway was just as silent as the dead server's corpse. I lifted the lid off of the cart and took a couple pieces of French toast off the plate. Having enough energy to run would prove helpful, if not essential, I knew.

I nearly jumped into the ceiling when an abrupt dinging noise sounded down the hallway. Instinctively, I dropped the toast and slumped against the wall, head down, pretending to be dead. If anyone else was still alive, I wanted to make sure they had no intentions of killing survivors before I alerted them to my presence. The elevator door opened but no one walked out. There was probably only a dead body on the floor of the elevator anyways. The doors closed again but the elevator didn't move.

Out of fear I laid on the floor for what felt like hours, just pretending to be dead, watching my French toast grow cold on the floor. By the time I found the courage to get off the floor my stomach was rumbling so loudly I expected it to alert everyone within a mile, assuming there was anyone alive within a mile. I picked up all of the French toast from the floor and the cart and headed to the staircase, not wanting to eat in front of the server's corpse. I ate the cold toast while sitting at the top of a concrete staircase in a cheap hotel in the Vatican. Sitting there, eating my toast in my utter solitude, I couldn't help but cry. I cried because there was nothing else to do. Nothing could bring back my fallen friends. Nothing could change what had happened, whatever that might have even been. I knew that everything would be different from that moment on.

I walked around the city blindly, just hoping to hear a human voice call out from somewhere. I knew where everyone was, it was Easter morning in Vatican City after all. It doesn't take a rocket scientist to know where all the people would be. I imagined the thousands of parishioners, all lying on the concrete, all dead.

At first, I avoided St. Peter's Square. I knew that thousands of bodies would be there and I didn't want to see it. I walked through the Old Gardens and past the Academy of Science, knowing that I had to get to St. Peter's Square eventually, just to sate my morbid curiosity. If anyone was still alive, the best chance was that I would find them in that throng of thousands. I came up behind St. Peter's Basilica and slumped against the building, not wanting to see the main square. Luckily, I had only passed a handful of corpses on my walk through the city. My friends and I, most likely being the only Lutherans in the whole of Vatican City on Easter, were one of the few groups that hadn't gone to the services.

After making the agonizing last steps to the front of St. Peter's Square, I was ready to look in at the carnage. Perhaps it was because I had already vomited so much earlier in the day, or perhaps I was already desensitized to the whole concept of death, but when I looked upon that ocean of still corpses, I didn't even blink. Bodies were everywhere. I called out for any survivors, but no one returned my desperate plea. Nothing moved, nothing made sound, everything was just perfectly still. It was as though everyone in the Square, all of the thousands of visitors and parishioners, had decided to simply go to sleep. The world was all dead. I started to wade through the bodies but there were too many. I had to walk around the edge of the crowd, towards the Sistine Chapel and the Apostolic Palace, pushing bodies out of my way, and I nearly made it to the front of the Basilica before my resolve broke and I cried again. I sat down against the wall, my feet pushing against the corpse of a little girl in a pink dress, her ears and eyes crusted with blood, and wept.

I jolted awake a few moments later to the sound of a low whirring noise, like a large ceiling fan had just been turned on over St. Peter's Square. Helicopters, I knew at once. I could hear the sound of helicopter blades cutting the air not far from my position. For a moment, I thought to stand and wave my arms. Then I panicked. What if these helicopters were filled with the same people who just caused this destruction? What if they were here to make sure the job was done, that everyone was dead?

A thousand ideas flew through my head as I collapsed back against the wall. Thinking it better to be cautious, I pulled the body of the little girl over my legs and lay as flat and still as I could, trying not to cough from the mounting stench or vomit from the feel of the girl's blood seeping out of her mouth and into the top of my shoe. I closed my eyes tight and tried to steady my breathing as best I could. I heard at least one helicopter land, right in the center of the throng of corpses. As it touched down, the weight of the helicopter crushed the bodies underneath it in a sickening squelch. The wet crunching sounds of the helicopter made me cough to hold back the French toast and keep it from splattering the ground. I could barely breathe.

I heard people getting out of the helicopter, all shouting to each other; I couldn't understand a word of their hurried Italian. Some of the voices got closer, some moved farther away. Then I heard one voice above the rest, obviously commanding the others, calling out in English. "My, oh my, boys! We sure have done ourselves a fine job this day, fine job indeed. Now, keep searching. I'm sure someone was bound to survive the effects, and we need to find them!" The voice sounded like Zachary Taylor striding into a saloon after the Battle of Buena Vista. The accent was unmistakable; it was an overly exaggerated Wild West fanatic who had stepped off of that helicopter to take charge of the scene.

After ten, maybe twenty minutes, the voices died down and the man with the old west accent, referred to by his compatriots only as "The Major", ordered everyone back on their helicopters and started to take off.

The wind from the helicopter blades as they passed overhead, right above the section of wall I was propped against, tossed a thick glob of congealed blood right onto my face and into my mouth. I started to cough and vomit again, hoping that the helicopter blades would cover the noise. I saw the end of the rotors clearing the Basilica and stood up to get the blood off of my body. Running out of St. Peter's Square as fast as I could and looking about frantically for signs to the subway, I couldn't help but think of all of the bodies I had just seen. Why would anyone want to kill all those innocent people? Was it a terrorist attack? What had happened? If the helicopters were going to stay in the area, I knew that I had to get underground. I made my way at a dead run to the Ottaviano subway station and bolted underground. "Safe," I whispered under my breath, "for now."

The subway was littered with more bodies. The dead were slumped over everywhere. I started walking along the tracks out of Vatican City and back into Rome. I had to get to the surface and see if anyone was still alive in Rome. I prayed that the world's population had not been reduced to just myself and the people after me.

As I made my way farther and farther down the subway tunnels I started to hear sirens. People were still very much alive above me. A wide smile broke out on my face at the realization that I wasn't the only person left. I climbed to the top of a subway exit, somewhere in Rome, and saw the stairs to the street barricaded. Two police officers were standing in front of the roped off staircase. So the police knew what had happened and had quarantined the area. Not having any ideas of how I would ever escape, I simply made a run for it. The officers were paying much more attention to the crush of people asking questions and shouting than to bother looking behind at the subway. It was terrifying to think that the officers had no expectations of any survivors coming out of Vatican City.

I bolted up the steps and leaped over the rope barrier, right in between the two policemen. The already loud crowd erupted as the officers began to yell and give chase. I heard one of them radio something and I knew that the chase would be on in full.

The crowd, too stunned to try and hold me back, simply stood aside as I darted through. The streets were packed with people, probably all trying to learn what happened to Vatican City. I heard the distinctive swoosh of helicopter blades above my head once more and ducked into an open air produce market, filled with people. Trying to act nonchalantly and blend in, I simply slowed my pace and began pretending to shop. Within a few short moments I heard the very clear voice of the one they called "The Major" yelling after me. I had been found.

Reaching down with my prosthetic arm I flipped over the small produce table I was standing near to create some commotion and bolted again. Fruits and vegetables fell everywhere, buying me time. I turned a sharp corner as I exited the market and saw a quaint café. My first thought was to simply sit down and pretend to have been there all morning. Even as the thought rushed through my head, I knew it wouldn't work. My prosthetic metal arm would give me away, especially in short sleeves. That's when I saw an older man getting up from his table, leaving his long coat on the chair. As I ran past the café I snatched up the jacket and threw it on, turning another corner onto a busy street full of traffic.

I could hear the voices of the police officers following me but I had gained some ground. Knowing I only had a few moments before the officers rounded the corner and saw me, I took a risk. I stopped, slowed my breathing as well as I knew how, and calmly walked up to the nearest taxi, opened the door, and got in. It was empty! Maybe I would get out of Rome after all, I thought. I told the driver to take me to the Leonardo da Vinci International Airport, terminal C, transatlantic. I still had my plane ticket in my pocket. As far as I knew, the authorities didn't know my name yet so I shouldn't be on any restricted flight lists.

My luck held out and I was able to get my ticket exchanged for the next flight back to America without anyone recognizing me. The passengers on the flight surprised me, not a single one of them mentioned anything about the catastrophe I just witnessed. A few times, I almost found the courage to ask a flight attendant if they had heard anything but I never could. Besides, I told myself, if anyone knew anything, they would be talking about it as much as they could, trying to get information.

The plane landed in the United States without incident and I made my way into the cold street to hail a cab. Where would I go? Would they be able to track me if I went back to my apartment? Could I simply fall back into my usual routine and live the rest of my life unnoticed? I got my answer soon enough.

I told the cab driver to take me to a bank near my apartment. If I was going to have to run again, I wanted to be prepared. "Heard anything about whatever happened in the Vatican? I saw something about it on the news when I landed in the airport." I hadn't actually seen any news reports, something I realized could get me in huge trouble if it hadn't been reported to the media yet.

"Nope. Nothing. What are you talkin' about anyways?" The cab driver glanced nervously at me in the mirror. Did he know? Had he been told? Had the police arranged for this specific cab driver to pick me up? How could they know where I was? I could feel the sweat starting to bead on my forehead.

"Oh nothing" I replied, "just heard something about the Pope misquoting the Bible or something during his sermon. Just curious, you know." I tried to play it off cool. I pulled out my phone and pretended to be texting someone for the rest of the cab ride. In truth, my phone had been dead for hours.

The cab driver slammed on the breaks suddenly and leapt out of the car, moving fast. I jerked my head up to see that we were not in front of a bank. It was a police station. That's when I noticed the black and white print out of my face taped to the steering wheel.

In a sheer panic I started to rip at the door handle. It was locked, of course. I pulled back my metal prosthetic arm and hit the window with all of my might. It sounded as if it loosened in the door but it didn't crack. I glanced over my shoulder and could see officers starting to come out of the police station. I hit the window again and breathed a slight sigh of relief when it started to crack. One more thunderous hit had the window falling to the ground, shattered.

I climbed through the window and hopped onto the street, ready to dash across the narrow road. I was jerked back violently when my stolen jacket caught on the broken glass still remaining in the door. I could hear it rip away from my shoulder so I simply put my feet against the hubcap and pushed forward, tearing the jacket off my body. I ran across the small road and into an alleyway between two townhomes. I leapt over a recycling bin and charged over a short chain link fence before looking back. Lady luck was with me again. The two officers that had come out of the station were not even close to capable of keeping up with my pace, fitting perfectly the stereotypical description of police being addicted to donuts and coffee. Each one of them was easily a hundred pounds heavier than my lithe, seventeen year old frame. I turned a few corners and ran on, a mile, maybe two miles, before I sat down in an alley with my back against a smelly brown dumpster.

Now I knew for sure that I was a wanted man. They had my stolen coat which they would no doubt be using to get hair samples and try figure out my identity. Thankfully, I still had my dead cell phone clutched in my hand. After seeing the carnage in Vatican City and knowing that the police who investigated the scene obviously caused the catastrophe and were proud of it, I was worried. I knew that if I was taken alive, I wouldn't stay that way for long. They would surely kill me without trial or even question. I had to take no risks. I set my phone on the pavement and bashed it to bits with my metal fist. I crumbled the sim card to powder and tossed the pieces into the dumpster. With this kind of pressure, I couldn't afford to accidentally lose it or have it captured. Holding my wallet in my hands, I knew that I had to destroy my driver's license as well. I tried in vain to crush it with my hand but it was too flexible. All I succeeded in doing was crumpling it and distorting the words.

Old memories played through my head, looking at the crumpled up driver's license. Mostly, I thought of my friends. I could see the faces of the dead in my mind. The bodies I had looted in the hotel room haunted me. I would never see any of them again. That was a different life, a different time.

Chapter 3

I waited in the alley for a few hours, relaxing with my head against the dumpster and listening, trying to hear the pursuit, if there was any. When night fell, it started to get cold. It wasn't quite winter yet, but winter was coming. I walked a few miles to the ghetto and it wasn't hard to find a trash can fire to stand beside and pretend I was just a runaway. The three hobos standing around the fire didn't even bother to say hello, they just kept staring into the flames as though there was some distant hope hidden within the fire that would reveal itself if you only looked long enough. I could see them all glance from time to time at my arm, but prosthetic limbs and amputees were common among the homeless. I doubt any of them had ever seen a metal arm quite like mine, but unlike the rich folk, the idea of a prosthetic limb didn't strike them as unusual, frightening, or grotesque.

One particular homeless man, appearing to be at least seventy years old, got up from his bench and made his way over to the barrel I was standing at. He was wearing a bright red heavy winter coat, or at least it was bright red at one point. The coat seemed to be at least as old as the wrinkled man wearing it. More interesting than the old red coat, the man was wearing a World War II veteran's hat over his stringy white hair. Pinned to the left of the text was a purple heart and pinned to the right was a silver star. He must have seen me eyeing his hat, for a wide smile broke out on his weathered face and he reached out his right hand. I returned the grin and shook his hand.

"Folks around here call me 'The Red Baron'; guess no one living out on the street really needs their own name. Once you've been sleeping on the cold ground, just doesn't make sense to go by the name your parents gave you." I knew I would fit right in as I tossed my driver's license into the fire and watched my old identity and life melt away.

"I'm Esau, nice to meet you." The name seemed fitting. If the government was bent on my destruction, than perhaps I would need some divine intervention to get out of this mess. The name brought some chuckles from my new homeless friends. I soon learned that my fireside companions were Ivan, a short man of average build with a scruffy beard and years of sadness in his eyes. Ivan, much to my surprise, was actually from Russia. His sister, whose name was so difficult to pronounce in English that everyone just called her Sarah, was born in the United States after their family had emigrated. Frank, who claimed to be a former male model before aliens stole his good looks and locked them inside a time capsule to use for genetic cloning on their home planet, had been born ultimately orphaned not far from where we now stood. The Red Baron was their leader and it seemed like a good group to join.

The next two days were thankfully uneventful. Our little band of five homeless people spent most of our days going to the various soup kitchens around the ghetto and we spent a good deal of time just walking around the streets. In my old life, living in a nice apartment after having finished school early, looking forward to an exciting life at college, I always looked down on the homeless as lazy people who just slept on park benches and under bridges all day. I couldn't have been more wrong. In just those two days the five of us managed to canvas the entire south side of the city. Red knew every single street, every alleyway, every soup kitchen and free food bank. In essence, Red knew this whole city. It was his city. Everyone who recognized him would politely tip their hat or nod, always showing nothing but respect for the old veteran.

The morning of the third day was different. I was curled up on the concrete beside the trash can fire, lying on a couple of old coats, when I heard Sarah scream. My eyes bolted up and I sat up on the ground. There they were: the police. They were grabbing Sarah, three officers dragging her to her feet and starting to haul her away. A fourth officer, a bit taller than the other three and with a voice of command that brokered authority, kept shoving a picture in front of Sarah's face, demanding that she tell them where the person in the photo was. Sarah just kept screaming that she didn't know who it was, she had never seen him, and she didn't understand what was going on. A police car rolled to a stop right behind the fighting group and the officers slammed Sarah's head down hard into the hood. As she went down she managed to squirm to the side and look right at me.

That look told me everything. It was my picture she was looking at. I started to get up slowly and move towards Red's bench. The cops didn't notice me as I crouched down behind the bench and shook the old man awake. I put my hand over his mouth to keep him from making noise as he startled back to consciousness. I pointed to the cop car and one of them noticed us. I slumped down, trying to disguise myself as a dirty pile of old clothes, a common ruse amongst the less fortunate, and I could hear the officer walking toward the bench.

"Hey, Red! You seen this kid? Probably about sixteen, maybe seventeen, runnin' away from home. Scared, nowhere to go, come on Red, you know everyone on the streets. Seen him?" There was a long pause. I could still hear Sarah struggling against the officers.

"You know I don't take runaways. This part of town is the old folk's area. Check one of the drop-in shelters. Or check down on 57th street with that young guy who runs things down there. You know, someone younger and more accessible, a young runaway would probably be hanging around somebody like that. I'll keep an eye out for our city's most wanted though." The Red Baron was protecting me. It didn't make sense. We had only known each other for three days. Well, we met three days ago. None of us really knew each other. No one talked much on our walks through the city, Red would just point things out and say the names of every street we passed.

"Okay, Red. You do that. You see this kid, you take him in. And then give us a call as soon as you can." He tossed a quarter onto the chest of my old homeless guardian. I couldn't tell if it was meant as an insult or if he honestly expected Red to go through the trouble of finding a working payphone and turning me in. "Also, I'm going to have to take your girl here down to the station for questioning." The officer said it without any hint of remorse or thought of sympathy. It was obvious that this was the way of it. When the cops came to the ghetto to get a homeless person, they just took whomever they wanted to take. Sarah started to put up a fight when the officers began to shove her into the back seat of the car. She kept fighting right until they clubbed her on the head with a nightstick.

Ivan kept to himself the entire next day, trying to fight back tears. It was clear to everyone that he loved his sister, his last remaining kin, very deeply. I sat next to him around the trash can fire and tried to think up some words I might offer as comfort. We didn't go walking that day. Frank went out and got us some food, even managed to come back with a half full bottle of cognac. We didn't ask where Frank got it, we just watched Ivan drink himself to sleep. Later that night Red sat me down on one end of his bench and told me about the police and what had happened.

"They come here every now and then, maybe half a dozen times a year." Red's eyes seemed to glaze over as he thought back on all of his years among the homeless. "They come and they rough us up and they ask about people, always people. Have we seen this person, have we heard about this one, where are we hiding this group of fugitives, it's always the same."

"This time was different," I managed to say. I knew that Red had recognized me from the picture.

"Yeah, you got that right. So, what did you do? Why are they after you? Why did I just watch my friend Sarah get taken by the police to protect you? It is about time I learned more about you, Esau." They way he talked about Sarah it was obvious that she wasn't coming back. I had gotten her killed.

I couldn't bring myself to look Red in the face, the guilt over Sarah was too much for me to bear. "You won't believe me if I told you. I swear though, I didn't do anything. I was just in the wrong place at the wrong time, and now the cops are after me. I wish I knew more about what was happening." I tried to say it with as much honesty as I could muster but as soon as the words left my mouth I realized how cliché it was. The wrong place at the wrong time, and now I'm a wanted man. It was probably the oldest story on the streets.

"Just like prison, kid. Everyone is innocent. We are all just victims of circumstance. That's alright for now though. I understand that it's hard to say you messed up." Red's eyes seemed to bore a hole through my soul.

"But you better watch out. When Ivan wakes up in the morning, you better be either ready to talk and explain yourself, or you better be gone. If he tries to kill you, I won't stop him. Just know that, kid." I didn't understand what the old man was saying at first. So, Red was willing to save me from the police, even at the expense of one of his friends, but when it came to justice within the group, homeless justice administered by the leader of the homeless, it was all or nothing. I either had to prove my case, or I would likely be killed. At least there was a sense of honesty and dignity about it. If I were to die during my street trial, at least I would die with honor.

Maybe it was just the rumbling in my stomach, maybe it was my nerves. My eyes never left Ivan the entire night as I tried to sleep. I just kept thinking about Sarah, his beloved sister, about the sorrow I had brought upon this close group of friends. I also kept wishing that Ivan had left enough cognac in the bottle for me to join him in his drunken slumber. Needless to say, I didn't get any sleep. I knew my story was too farfetched to be believable. I couldn't prove anything.

I still don't know how I found the nerve to stay that night. I could have easily walked off in the middle of the night and found some other place to sleep and live. Something about the way that they had protected me the previous day kept me from running. They had risked their lives to save a stranger, I owed them the honesty of my story. Knowing beyond certainty that if I ran away, none of them would say a word about it, I just sat there, huddled up against the cold chill of night, watching the fire dwindle down, watching Ivan sleep. Every few minutes I would look to the spot where Sarah used to sleep, closest to the fire, and I would think about running away. I was ashamed of myself when the sun rose. I couldn't even find the strength to shed a single tear for our lost friend.

The morning came too soon. The Red Baron was the first to wake up. "It's time to talk, Esau" he said as he woke Frank and Ivan from their sleep. We all sat around the fire on the dirty concrete and I told my story. I told them all about the trip to the Vatican, the strange vibrations, the deaths of my closest friends. I told them about running through the streets and escaping back to America. I knew there was no possible way that any sane person would believe what I had just said.

"Come on, let's find a T.V. and see if we can watch the news. Even with a cover up, that many people dead can't be hidden for long. It has to have made the news by now. That will prove my story." It was my only hope. None of the others had said a word through my whole story. They just kept looking at Ivan, watching his rage build. He had lost a sister, likely the only family he had left, and it was all to save me, a kid they hardly knew. We started walking down the street, heading toward a café that Red knew had screens visible from the street.

"Look, the morning news is playing right now. They have to be talking about it. Something like this will be the most deaths in a single day since Noah escaped the flood." I was amazed. We watched the news for almost an hour without a single mention of Vatican City. There was nothing. Not a single word about the thousands of people slaughtered on Easter morning. Nothing. How could anyone have covered up such a massive killing? It would take years to plan and execute a slaughter of the magnitude I had seen. Or had it all just been in my head? Am I insane? The news report left me with more questions than answers.

I tried to remember everything that had happened before I went to Vatican City. I remembered things like facts, my name, my school, my age, things that I *knew* to be true, but when I tried to recall the events just before I got off the plane in Rome and went to my hotel, I couldn't. I stood there, staring at the news channel, trying to remember what had happened right before my friends died. I was in a hot tub, I knew that. I couldn't remember it thought, I only knew it as though it were some piece of memorized mathematics fact. I shook my head, wondering if it had been me who caused all of that destruction and death. It couldn't have been, I told myself in disbelief.

We left the café in silence. "I say we kill him," Ivan announced as soon as we returned to our camp. Red sat down on his bench. Frank just looked away. Ivan bent over and pulled out a crudely made shank from his boot.

"Wait, we can fix this." I put my hands up, trying to look as harmless as possible, backing away from the grimacing man. "If we all work together, maybe we can rescue Sarah. We have to at least try. Killing me will only hurt the group. We have to stick together to stay strong. One less person will only diminish our chances of success." It was a desperate plea from the mouth of a desperate man.

Luckily, it seemed as though my logic was working. Red and Frank both looked my direction. They were interested in the plan that was brewing in my mind. Ivan didn't buy it though. He lunged at me, the shank aiming right at my gut.

I got my right arm down just in time to block the stab, twisting my hips to the side and creating a smaller target. The cheap aluminum of the blade bent considerably against the steel and carbon fiber of my prosthetic arm. I brought my arm up in a quick jerking motion that sent the shank flying to the ground. "Look, I'm stronger than I seem," I said, trying to diffuse the situation. "This arm isn't like any usual prosthetic. It was an experiment. My uncle was an engineer for the military." Ivan stood there, staring at me, his mouth slightly agape.

"When I lost my arm, he made this for me. That's why this plan can work. We can fight back!" I thought for a moment of standing on the bench to make my impromptu speech. "We can go to the police station and find Sarah before it's too late. Now, who is with me?" My speech, while not the most rousing call to arms in history, worked. Red was on his feet, Frank was smiling and patting Ivan on the shoulder, and Ivan himself even seemed intrigued. It was settled. Four homeless guys were about to storm a police station and rescue our friend. "When you have nothing left to lose, every risk becomes nothing but reward waiting to be taken

Chapter 4

"The first thing we have to do is find a good source of methane. My arm is powered by the compressed gas. My arm receives the electrical signals from my brain that are sent along wires to a tiny computer that controls the release of methane. The carbon fiber muscles then contract and expand according to the amount of gas released. I'm not that close to running out, but if we are going to take a police station by force, I want it to be full, might have to do some heavy lifting in there. I usually get my shipments of methane in the mail from my uncle once every three months. He lives across the country though, so we can't just ask him for more. Anyone have any bright ideas?"

"There is a chemical lab on the east side of town, Schwartz Laboratories or something like that, we could break in there and see if they have it." Frank said eagerly.

"A place like that probably has security cameras. We need to stay off the grid as long as possible if we are going to make this crazy plan work." The Red Baron was right. We couldn't just break into a sophisticated laboratory and get away without being pursued.

"Maybe we could hit one of their trucks about to make a delivery?" Ivan suggested.

"Ivan here did some time up state for grand theft a while back. If he still has the skills," Ivan was smiling at the idea, "that might just work."

"Or it might get us all killed if the driver is carrying a gun, don't forget that. If we are going to steal this methane, I would rather it not involve the possibility of getting shot or leaving witnesses that would turn us in." From the tone of his voice it sounded like Frank had some experience in the business of robbery and he wasn't eager to try it again.

"Regardless of what we decide to do, we need to first locate the methane. We should head out and do some surveillance.

If we can figure out if this place even has it, than we can make a real plan to break in and get it." We started walking east in the direction of the laboratory, everyone thinking of Sarah and our duty to get our friend back.

The laboratory was a huge brick complex. Barbed wire fences surrounded the entire compound and a small guard shack overlooked the entrance. The place looked like an old munitions factory that had been turned into a prison. "Must be some pretty secret stuff in there," I said, looking at the defenses with despair. "No reason to have all those guards walking around if all they do is make some household chemicals. When was the last time you saw this place, Frank?" He looked just as surprised as the rest of us.

"Just a month or so ago. I was meeting someone down here to trade a pair of gloves for some cigarettes. The fence, the guard shack, the armed patrols, those weren't here. This place looked just like a normal business. All of this security is new. I don't like this place. We shouldn't be here." Frank started to turn around and walk away before Red caught him on the arm.

"For Sarah's sake, we need to stay a little longer and figure this place out." Red seemed just as nervous as the rest of us.

"The back half of the building looks new. You can see the marks left by the excavation equipment," I observed. "They dug out a huge chunk of the hillside to build the addition. We should get up there so we can check this place out from above." I was more curious than scared, I realized. The couple of guards standing near the gate and looking our way got everyone moving. We took a wide path out to the east of the complex and circled our way to the top of the newly excavated hill.

The laboratory was built somewhat on the edge of the city, in one of the more forested areas. This section of town was just being developed, new businesses moving in, streets and parking lots being paved. There was even a large parking garage across the street from Schwartz Laboratories that was intended to serve a planned shopping mall in the area. All of the development had come to a halt when the market went bad.

What we saw from the top of the hill was amazing. Lying on our stomachs in the dense underbrush of the knoll, we were able to see the entire complex from a bird's eye view. The older brick structure was larger, much larger, than it appeared from the ground. The most intriguing part was the newest addition. Set into the newly excavated land, the back half of the building was a modern steel behemoth. The top of the building was arched like an old gothic cathedral and was complete with flying buttresses of black steel. The steeply sloping sides of the arched roof had large panels of glass set into it, presumably as skylights. Why would a chemical laboratory have hired armed guards, invested heavily in physical security, and then built a gothic cathedral out of black steel? None of it made any sense. The four of us just crouched there on the hill for a long while, taking it all in.

"We should get some binoculars and see if we can look through those skylights and get some idea of this place before we go in," I said, pointing to the high windows. I wanted to get a clear picture of this strange place before I risked my life trying to invade it.

"Better yet, why don't we just go down and pick the lock on that door? I haven't seen any of the guards come by this section of the building lately and nothing has happened at the back door." Frank produced a small lock picking set from inside his coat and started to make his way to the edge of the hill.

"Esau, you go with Frank," Red said calmly, like he had done this sort of thing a hundred times before. "You are the fastest and can get out easiest if something goes wrong. Ivan and I will stay up here and play lookout. If you hear a whistle, get out. Got it?"

"Yeah, I got it" I said with a shake of my head. I couldn't believe I was going in blind to a highly guarded chemical laboratory. Frank and I slid down the rocky slope, trying to be as stealthy as possible. We hit the bottom with only a few minor scrapes and cuts from the rocks and roots along the hillside and quickly moved to the door. Frank was an expert. He had the door unlocked in ten seconds flat. Much to my surprise, Frank turned around and started to climb back up the hill before even opening the door.

"Frank! What are you doing?" I whispered, frantically looking around to see if any of the guards had seen us and were coming.

"Cold feet," Frank said with a shrug of shoulders. "Have fun in there." I was on my own.

I pushed the door open as slowly as possible, expecting to hear the shouts of guards or the rush of air as bullets passed my head. Thankfully, all I heard was silence. I let the door swing wide and slipped in behind it to get my bearings.

The inside of the strange cathedral was almost completely empty. The floor was made of some sort of cool, black stone and the walls were equally dark. The only light came from a pair of small chandeliers hanging from the ceiling. A solitary man was in the room, standing by himself, looking right at me. He was an incredibly old man, older than Red by what seemed to be centuries, and he was wearing a simple black robe with a rope around the waist. The old man stood in front of a podium facing the door I had just come through. There was a massive book opened on the podium before the old man but he wasn't looking at it. He was staring right at me. The mouth of his old and wrinkled face was moving, but he wasn't speaking.

Without taking my eyes off the old man, I lunged toward the door. He didn't move. His eyes followed me but he made no other motion. His mouth just kept moving as though he was silently speaking, reciting some poem he had memorized thousands of years before. I reached for the door but then stopped and turned back.

There were two other doors in the room, one right behind the old man, I assumed it would lead into the normal section of the laboratory because it was made of modern metal and glass. The other door was set into the wall on my left and looked like it was made of marble taken directly from the palace of some long dead king. Above that door was the inscription *"Lux in Tenebris"* and the word *"Petra"* was carved into the door itself. None of it made any sense. I didn't know the words and the spookiness of the dimly lit room was playing with my mind.

I moved toward the marble door and reached a hand up to touch the carving, always watching the man in the center of the room. As soon as my hand touched the door his head snapped around to look directly at me. His mouth stopped moving and he simply stood there, watching me. That's when I noticed that his eyes were completely devoid of anything but white. They were so ridden with cataracts that it was impossible for him to see. The old man was utterly blind.

I backed away from the door and stood in the center of the room, my arms out to the sides unthreateningly, my nerves on edge. Immediately, the man began staring straight ahead and his mouth moved again. I walked slowly to the other door, the normal door, and found it unlocked. The old man didn't seem to care when I opened it and stepped through. I was at the back of a normal looking, modern, chemical laboratory. The bright white lights were a stark contrast to the dimly lit cathedral room I had just left and it took my eyes a moment to adjust. I could hear the sounds of computers and employees going about their work farther ahead. Trying to be a stealthy as possible, I walked as quickly as I could down the stark hallway. I turned a corner and found two more doors. One was labeled "Control Room" and the other, much to my surprise, was labeled as a supply closet.

I thanked my lucky stars and rejoiced in how easy it was to steal the supplies I needed. With a rather large canister of compressed methane gas tucked under my arm, I made my way back to the cathedral room. I opened the door and found it exactly as I had left it. Curiosity overcame my logical reasoning and I glanced over the old man's shoulder as I walked past to see the book on the podium. As though the strangeness of the building would never end, I found that the book was blank. Both of the pages displayed before the man were totally blank, although the pages looked like they might be even older than the man standing behind them. Adding to my confusion, when I walked out of the door at the back of the room, I got the most terrifying surprise yet. I climbed back up the hill to where my friends were supposed to be waiting for me and found no sign of them at all. They were simply gone. It didn't look like there was any sort of struggle and there were no footprints in the area. They had simply vanished.

I wasn't sure if they had been captured by the guards, killed, or if they had simply left. Nothing made sense. It was impossible to think that the few minutes I had spent in the laboratory was enough to cause them to impatiently leave. I walked back to the area of dirty concrete that we called home and saw my three friends sitting around the trash can fire, thoroughly amazed to see me. I was thankful they were alive.

"What? Why did you guys leave me there? What happened?" They didn't say anything, they just kept staring. "What happened?" I asked again as I looked to Frank, fear edging my voice.

"Esau... You were gone for seven days. We thought you were dead."

Chapter 5

"Well, at least I got what I went in for. You guys won't believe that place though. The longer I was in there, the weirder it all got, although I couldn't have been in there more than half an hour." My mind was racing, trying to put the pieces together, trying in vain to make sense of the bizarre experience.

Red just shook his head. "Something very strange is going on here," the old man said with a sigh. "The cops came back twice since you've been gone, asking about you. They still haven't figured out who you are, but they are after you for sure. Plus, now some Fed is rolling along with them, probably FBI from the looks of his suit. They call him 'The Major', found it kind of funny that a guy called The Major would come poking around the territory of The Red Baron."

"Yeah, the Major, I've seen him before. He was one of the ones leading the group of officers that inspected the massacre at Vatican City. As far as I can tell, he runs the whole operation and he wants me dead." I still didn't understand anything that was going on. "We need to get back into that lab, all of us," I said, trying to sound as determined as I could despite my fears. "They are doing something down there and I think it has to do with the massacre. Maybe we can figure out what their whole operation is and come up with a plan to expose them to the real authorities or else take them down ourselves."

"Unless the entire US government is behind it all! We can't trust anyone now. We're on our own," Ivan yelled, making the rest of us laugh. Ivan loved conspiracy theories. Growing up during the end of the Cold War in Soviet Russia can have profound effects on a young mind.

"Oh, come on, Ivan, you still think the ballots from each election are sent on a space shuttle to the moon so no one knows they aren't counted! Someone in the government might be covering this whole thing up, but I would bet that the higher levels of government have no idea what is happening." Red was at least making sense, like usual.

"So what should we do next? We need to make a plan. Do we go in?" I asked, looking to the Red Baron for answers. Red seemed to know the most about this kind of thing, being a war veteran, and from the looks of it, a hero as well.

"First things first, we need to get supplies. Frank, you still know that fence who hangs out down on Vine Street? He should be able to get everything we need."

Frank's face suddenly went pale. "I don't think we will have time for that. Plans are changing, time to go!" The four of us turned around in unison to see the patrol car rolling up on us. Within a few seconds we were all on our feet running, shouts of pursuit following us closely.

"There he is! Catch that kid! Keep him alive until I have him!" It was the voice of the Major, without a doubt. He had personally come to capture me and from the sound of it, he was interested in eventually putting my homeless life to a miserable end. I grabbed the bottle of methane I had stolen and pressed the nozzle to the small port above my elbow, feeling the gas fill the reservoir in my arm. It took just a few seconds to fully fill the chamber and I tossed the half full canister back behind me with a smile, aiming for the smoldering fire in the trash can and I ran with all my heart.

The electrical nerves attaching the arm to my brain registered the full capacity of the methane storage area under my skin. I flexed my arm as I ran, feeling the new found power and relishing it.

Judging by the loud explosion, my diversion worked. The methane canister exploded right in front of the patrol car and hopefully bought us some time. Not thirty yards into our run, Red started to fall behind. It was obvious that he was too old for this sort of thing. I grabbed him by the arm and started to drag him along, using my strength to boost his speed. "They only want me," I yelled. "Split away and go with the others to hide. I'll come find you later." The look of sadness and desperation in the Red Baron's face was enough to break my heart. It was obvious that he wanted more than anything to just help me. He didn't know what to do and it looked like he might cry out of helplessness. I put the image out of my mind and veered off to my left, down an alley littered with trash.

I could hear the rest of our group running down the sidewalk and the sounds of the officer's feet following down the alley. At least the rest of them were likely to escape. I jumped up onto a closed dumpster and reached for the ledge of the nearest roof. Feeling the brick beneath my fingertips, I locked my prosthetic arm firmly into place on the edge and used my inhuman strength to pull myself up. I felt a dull thud against the back of my coat and looked back to see an officer kneeling and holding something aimed at my back that looked suspiciously like a gun.

Rolling over the ledge I reached around my back and felt the leads of the taser lodged in the thick fabric of the old jacket. I grabbed them and ripped them out, tossing them aside as I ran. I got lucky there. A concentrated electric shock to anywhere in my body would probably detonate the compressed methane gas stored in my metallic prosthetic.

I ran across the rooftops of the old buildings along the street, my footfalls pounding loudly on the slate, jumping over the small ledges that marked the boundaries of each one. I could see my friends still running along the sidewalk on the other side of the street. Ivan was looking up at me, watching my run. I motioned for him to take the next turn off to the right and the group did. They stopped there, the officers having lost interest in them and turning their full attention to my capture.

I saw two cops running along the ground, pushing pedestrians out of their way with reckless abandon, paralleling my path above them. Looking over my shoulder, I glanced back quickly enough to see three other officers giving chase on the rooftops. To my left was nothing but open ground, the ruins of an abandoned factory that had been demolished decades ago. The only rooftops in reach were all in a straight line, right before me. I knew I couldn't separate the two groups of pursuing officers easily. Fear started to fully set in as I realized the rooftops ended in two blocks. I would have to jump down to the street.

I put my legs in motion as fast as they could possibly run, hoping to put some distance between us before I reached the end of the buildings. The officers were just as relentless. I was only two, maybe three small rooftops ahead of the officers when I came to the end of the line. There was a steel beam with a long arm extending over the intersection, holding the stoplights, just a few feet from the edge of the building.

I looked back at my pursuers and made my decision. Steeling my nerves and mustering my courage, I leaped out to the beam, clearing the terrifying gap over the sidewalk. I used my strong arm to grab over the top of the beam and swung my body around the pole, landing on the arm with the stoplights, straddling it painfully. The officers were at the edge of the last rooftop by the time I steadied myself, looking hesitantly at the beam. I smiled to them, waved, and let go of the beam, dropping directly on top of a large delivery truck that had just started to move as the lights turned green. It was only a two or three foot drop from where I was sitting on the pole so the driver didn't even notice the sound of his new cargo. The truck picked up speed and left the officers behind, staring at me with malice in their eyes.

I waited a few blocks before I dropped off the top of the truck and onto the hard pavement. Now what? Should I go back and make sure everyone else was alright? Would the police be waiting for me, expecting that I would do exactly that? A thousand questions ran through my head. The risk was too high, I finally decided. If I went back to the alley where I saw Red and the others hide and the cops were waiting for me, it would likely be the death of all of us. I had to wait it out on my own. The Major knew I was living with the homeless for sure now so I couldn't go to any of the free food soup kitchens like usual, they would be watching without a doubt. I still had the couple hundred dollars in my pocket from Italy, and I decided to spend some of it.

My first stop was a pawn shop. It took almost half an hour, but after considerably haggling and some slight bribery I convinced the pawn shop owner to take me out behind the building and show me the unregistered guns. I didn't have much cash, but street weapons were always cheap. After convincing the shop keeper to sell me bullets as well, I took my newly acquired revolver, secured it inside a deep pocket in my winter coat, and headed for a warm meal at a nice restaurant. After the first two establishments I went to turned me out for my appearance, I finally was able to pay a hostess a few dollars to let me sit at the bar and eat. Well under the drinking age, it took even more cash to order a beer.

At the end of the night I counted out my remaining funds, likely the last money I would ever see. I had a little less than two hundred dollars left to my name.

In the long run, the meal and the beer weren't necessary to my survival, so I shouldn't have wasted so much money. There is something about sitting at a bar with real people, people with houses, people with families, that makes a person feel human again. Even though I had been on the street for only what seemed to be a few days, I felt like I had been homeless my whole life. I looked homeless, I certainly smelled homeless, and I ate at shelters and charity missions. Everywhere I went I was greeted by little children staring in wonder, pointing their fingers. The people old enough to understand that I was a homeless kid just turned their faces away.

It was as though the whole world was ashamed of me. Being in that fancy restaurant, sitting next to totally normal people, eating good food, it wasn't important to my physical survival, but it was critical to my humanity. Having a prosthetic limb, especially a metal one, is dehumanizing enough. Being homeless? That's worse. So I sat at that bar for a couple hours, drinking my solitary beer, eating while trying not to make eye contact with anyone.

I couldn't help but hear the voice of my mother in my head, reading the Bible to me late at night, hearing her explain the verses one at a time. "The King will reply, 'Truly I tell you, whatever you did for one of the least of these brothers and sisters of mine, you did for me.'" I would mutter the line under my breath whenever a waitress or bartender asked if I needed anything. They always sneered when they spoke to me, like I was some large vermin in their precious restaurant, poisoning the food and the atmosphere for everyone else.

There were TVs at the bar too. Most of them were showing a horse race, but a small few were playing a news channel. I watched those TVs like a hawk. Nothing was ever mentioned about Vatican City. Not even a mention about the content of the Pope's Easter address, of course he never got to give one. So, whoever was behind this whole thing was keeping it quiet, but so far not offering any sort of counter story at all. Surely all those parishioners and tourists from around the world would be missed by now! Their families should be crying out in outrage! Why has there been a void of news coverage?

Early the next morning I went back to my usual spot in search of my unlikely group of comrades. They were there, the three that remained, all asleep, the trash can fire barely a heap of smoldering coals. I laid down on my designated spot of hard concrete and fell asleep beside them all. I was still homeless, but something about that meal and that bar made me feel human again. Everyone smiled when we woke up, but none of them smiled as much as I did.

Chapter 6

"I want this kid and I want him now! How hard can it be to catch a seventeen year old homeless kid with a shiny metal arm? Come on people. Your performance disgusts me." The Major was yelling at the top of his lungs. A flying object accented every word. Pen holders, keyboards, trashcans, everything in the small precinct became airborne as the Major's violent tornado of anger swept over the desks.

"Sir, Major… Sir, perhaps… If we knew *why* you-" The veteran cops leaning against the bulletin board at the back of the room shook their heads. The new guys fresh out of the academy always broke the cardinal rule. It was even written in the bathroom on a stall in thick black ink: Do not, under any circumstance, speak to the Major when he is speaking. It was a simple rule, really. When the Major opened his mouth, all other mouths in the room should close. The rookies never took it seriously. They usually didn't screw up this badly though.

The tirade stopped momentarily as the Major looked directly at the foolish young cop, hatred seething behind his eyes. The new cop visibly shrank back in his chair, appearing as insignificant as possible, staring intently at the floor.

"Major, please, if I may," the old police chief said. He usually knew how to calm him down, "the lad just wants to know why in God's name we are going out into the ghetto looking to arrest some teenage kid! He hangs around with the Red Baron for Christ's sake. How long has that old man been informing for us? Are you willing to risk that kind of asset for a kid? If the Baron says this kid isn't causing any trouble, there is no reason not to believe him. Now, maybe if you could provide us with some hard evidence, maybe just enough so we could legally arrest this kid, maybe then, we would be more enthusiastic about going out there and getting him."

"Since when does any of that matter?" the Major roared. "When have you boys cared about the law and legal arrests? This kid is a homeless degenerate, wanted for *murder* in Europe. It's our job to go out there and get him off the street before he kills again!" Everyone in the room fell silent at that. No one had suspected that murder was the charge being leveled against the kid.

"Major… what kind of force do you want us to use to bring this kid in?" There was a new level of respect in the police chief's voice as he said it, mindlessly toying with the leather holster of his gun.

"Use everything. Burn the damned ghetto to the ground if you must. Red is so old he won't be an informant for you much longer anyways. If you have to kill him, do it, do it without hesitation. Bring everything to bear on this case. We need to get this kid before he attacks someone again. We don't know why he kills, just that he kills without remorse and he does it very effectively." The Major was spinning a beautiful web of lies, trapping everyone in it. "We don't know if Red is in on it or any of those other guys, they could all be part of some larger conspiracy, we have no idea. This thing could be tied to some street gang, or even as high up as a corporate syndicate." The Major had the attention of everyone in the room. Some officers even bothered to take notes.

"His crimes in Europe all happened in Italy," the Major continued, "so we aren't ruling out Italian mob activity either. It seems unlikely since he is just a kid, but we know that most soldiers start young. My guess is that this kid is either Russian or Italian mafia, a soldier, newly recruited for a job the mob knew would be suicide." Police officers working in the city always loved a sensational story about the mafia. The Major had them. "He did the job, lived to tell it, and went rogue when his boss tried to kill him. We don't think his targets have been anyone connected yet, but we can't rule it out. He may be working up the mob hierarchy and taking down the whole organization." The Major smiled, even managing to bend over and pick up a coffee mug he had knocked off a desk.

"I say we just let him go then, this kid can do our job for us." The rookie cop dared to speak again, grinning and looking around to the other officers for support. None came.

"That's exactly what my boss wants. Captain Bill McCreary wants us to just watch this thing play out, see if the kid starts to target anyone we don't want dead ourselves. We can't do that though. As soon as the media gets wind of all this and figures out we have done nothing, they will burn the entire police organization to the ground with their articles. Don't forget, we run on taxpayer money. The media controls the taxpayers. We have to bring him in and we have to do it quick." It didn't take long for the entire station to agree. This kid was a threat to the public and needed to be brought down, whatever the cost. During the entire rousing speech, the Major just kept smiling to himself. He was always a good public speaker and knew exactly what to do to get the smaller precincts to come under his control. Without offering any proof, evidence, anything remotely substantial, he was able to get the entire precinct out on the streets to do his bidding. Yes, the Major thought, he should have been a politician. No, not a politician, the Major thought to himself. A king. He should have been born a king.

"I'm going back to headquarters. I expect to see this kid in handcuffs before the end of the week. No exceptions." With that, the Major left the precinct. He got into his old, beat up and rusty town car and started to drive into the ghetto. He never took his fancy cars, or his police uniform for that matter, into the rougher parts of town. It didn't take long to make it to Red's part of town. There was the kid, sitting on that bench, right next to the Red Baron. How easy it would be to stop the car, get out, and put a bullet in his head and end this whole fiasco. No, he couldn't do it, he reminded himself. After that last stunt with the exploding fire barrel, he knew he couldn't go alone, so he just drove right on past. The police would do their work, he knew. Besides, the Major thought, better that the local cops take the bullets than him.

He drove past the bench twice more that night, always watching the kid, never being conspicuous. He finally stopped the car outside a small pub, deep in the ghetto. It was time to try and get some answers and see who this kid was.

It took less than an hour to figure out that everyone in the ghetto knew Red and none of them were willing to talk about him. The Red Baron was some sort of folk hero to the homeless and downtrodden. The Major finished his schnapps, paid his tab, and made his way back to his car, still knowing nothing about the kid he was after. He drove back out of the ghetto heading east and parked in the small parking structure across from Schwartz Laboratories. After waiting a while in the car to make sure no one was following or watching him, the Major got out and made his way across the street to the gatehouse that overlooked the entrance to the lab.

"Nice to see you sir, welcome," the guard said stiffly. It was a practiced response that the Major had heard a hundred times before. Everyone here feared him and respected him, just like the Major liked it. None of the guards would look at him more than to confirm his identity. The gate slowly swung open and the Major walked briskly forward, heading toward the main entrance. The two guards to the sides of the gatehouse fell into step beside him as he made his way up the concrete path. The guard on his right opened the door and the guard on his left saluted as the Major walked through.

The inside of the front of the laboratory was just like anyone would expect. A pretty receptionist sat behind a large desk with several computer monitors on it and she looked up and smiled as the Major walked up to her. The Major didn't like pretty girls, especially this one. She reminded him too much of his Sheila, his wife. She was pretty once, the Major remembered, much prettier than the young blonde behind the desk.

"Good evening, sir. Welcome to Schwartz Laboratories. Should I inform Dr. Kowalski that you are here and wish to see him?" She was polite enough, albeit annoying. The secretary had been working the front desk of Schwartz Laboratories for years now; she shouldn't even bother to say anything more than 'welcome' when the Major walked in. He was always grumpy; didn't everyone know that by now? The fewer words spoken to the Major, the happier he would be.

Without so much as a glance at the young secretary, the Major said something that came out only as an angered growl and continued down the hallway.

The grumbling man walked down the corridor to the office with Kowalski's name on it and opened the door. He never knocked when he was at the lab. In fact, the Major rarely knocked anywhere he went. Kowalski was sitting behind his enormous, solid oak desk, writing something. The Major collapsed into one of the two cushy leather chairs opposite Kowalski's desk, waiting for him to finish his writing. If the Major could be said to have any real friends, Dr. Kowalski was it. They had known each other since they were little, even attended the same college together.

"And to what, exactly, do I owe this unexpected pleasure, Major?" Kowalski always had a dry way of speaking that indicated beyond a doubt that he preferred his chemistry and physics to the pleasantries of human companionship. He glanced up just once to make sure it actually was the Major sitting across from him before going back to his papers and his reports.

"I trust you have heard, the operation in Vatican City was a success," the Major said dryly, almost sounding bored as he looked around the room, reading some of the book titles on the shelves.

"I assume that we left none to question the events of that day?" Kowalski finished writing and stacked his papers together before sliding them into a desk drawer and locking the drawer shut.

"That's exactly why I am here," the Major said, frowning and glancing around the room. "It seems there has been one loose end. A kid, maybe seventeen or eighteen years old, he was alive in Saint Peter's Square when we landed to inspect the results. We chased him, but the kid can run. He got away and has ended up back here, right in this very city. It seems to be nothing more than a pure coincidence, but we cannot afford to take chances here." The Major considered his own words for a moment, never having given the possibility that the kid was chasing *him* much thought. Had it just been luck that brought the only survivor back to the Major's own hometown?

"A survivor? Impossible!" Kowalski shouted in a rare outburst. "No one should have survived that. Everything we know about the artifact says that no survivors should have been left. Are you sure he didn't just wander into the square after it happened?" Kowalski seemed nervous now. His voice was starting to shake as he spoke. "Even if he did happen upon the carnage, he has to be eliminated! We can't allow any witnesses if our plan is to succeed!" Dr. Kowalski ran his hand through the stringy remnants of his balding hair, a nervous tick he had all his life.

"Do you think I don't know that already? We have been chasing this kid for a week now. He is living with the homeless on the other side of town, west of here. Don't worry Kowalski, this will all be taken care of soon enough." The Major tried to calm him down but in truth, he was just as worried. "We know he told his homeless friends about what he saw, but so far I am confident that he has no idea what really happened. All he knows is that everyone inside Vatican City died, everyone except him. The local police managed to capture one of his buddies, a female, and before she died we learned everything we could about what the kid thinks and how he is operating. He isn't some sort of professional mastermind, not even close. We should have him in custody before the week is out, even with those incompetent local cops handling it. Trust me Kowalski, we have nothing to worry about."

"Your words do little to comfort me. Keep me informed about these developments. I want to know the moment he is captured. I might even enjoy watching his interrogation." Dr. Kowalski managed to smile despite the grim news.

"But of course. You know I will always keep you up to date on everything. All I ask is that you do the same. How goes your research?" Kowalski seemed to have calmed down and the two were speaking as friends again, leaning back in their chairs.

"Stubbornly slow. Keeping all of this operation under the radar for so long creates a huge barrier to my work. There are supplies I need that I am unable to order, places I would like to travel to for my research, you understand these things. It's hard to conduct research on such an important subject while trying to keep things secretive. If I could call in a few other scholars, get their opinions, things would go much quicker." It all made sense. Even a liberal arts history guy like the Major could understand that running a scientific research project completely isolated and secret would be difficult and time consuming. Still, it had to be done. Precautions were necessary.

"Time is running out, Kowalski. I want our little artifact to be understood fully within a month. I've given you enough time already to unlock its mysteries." The Major wasn't agitated, just trying to urge Kowalski on, like an old friend might challenge someone to a new goal. There had always been a healthy amount of competition between the two. "I know that part of the program will take some time. Now, what of the formula I asked you to make, progress I hope?"

"Yes, yes, the bomb that will incinerate a whole city. That part is easy. I have essentially recreated a World War Two British fire bomb. You could drop it on Dresden and no one would know the difference. The tricky part comes in making the chemical signatures appear to be Middle Eastern. Don't misunderstand me, I know the mission fully and agree that it has to be done with utmost haste, it is just taking longer than I thought." Dr. Kowalski was always a perfectionist. Everything had to be just right before he would move forward with any project or plan.

"An explosion this big will certainly attract the attention of the world's foremost chemists, myself among them," he gave a slight wink as he said it, "I just have to make sure the formula for the accelerant is believable for the story. The types of compounds I am used to working with don't show up much outside of the United States, much less the third world Muslim theocracies that we are trying to pin this on. Surely, you understand."

"I do, I do. I know that to make it perfect, it will take time. I'm just not so sure how long it will be before our hourglass has run empty." The Major and Kowalski both knew that a survivor narrowed their window of opportunity greatly. "Don't forget, we have a few thousand bodies to incinerate. My team has worked tirelessly, night and day, to cover this thing up. It's a massive operation, don't forget. The sooner we can get this explosion to Vatican City, the better chance of success we have." The Major started to stand as he finished speaking. He reached his arm and shook Kowalski's hand as he left the room.

"I know, I understand fully. Your sense of urgency isn't lost upon me. Trust me Major, I am working as fast as possible on this. You should expect the formula to be completed within the week and the device ready for delivery within a fortnight. My physicists are the best the world has to offer since Einstein's day. In fact, if you could find any of those old Jewish scientists looking for asylum still, feel free to send them my way. My people still believe they are working on predicting a terrorist chemical weapons delivery system, I'm not sure how long they will blindly follow us!" Kowalski chuckled at the notion as the Major, a huge smile on his face for the first time in probably months, walked out the door.

The Major sauntered down the plain white hallway through the laboratory and into the back of the building. The old man at the podium always managed to send a shiver through his spine. Whenever he looked upon that wrinkled heap of flesh and bones he always thought back to when he found him, tucked away in a hidden cave on the side of Mount Hor, naked and older than the mountain itself, just sitting in the dark cave, reading his blank book. It hadn't taken long to bribe the Jordanian government and within two days of finding him, the old man was clothed in a plain robe and standing at his podium, always reading.

The Major stood before the man at the podium and simply watched him read for a long moment, wondering what could have once been printed on the crinkled pages. "Have one of the acolytes come up to speak with me." The old man stopped his silent reading and turned his head towards the stone door and closed his eyes. After about a minute, the door slowly opened and another robed man, seemingly an exact replica of the one behind the podium, steeped forward on withered legs. "How fast do you age down there? I swear, last week you were no more than thirty. You look two hundred and thirty now." The Major was clearly unnerved. "So, any news? Have you unlocked all of its mysteries? Can I go down and safely see it?"

In a voice that seemed to tremble out of fear and at the same time possessed a steadiness that comes from knowing confidence, the old acolyte replied, "I would not recommend that, sir. I am afraid that we are no closer now than we were all those years ago when we first started. This mystery is more profound than you could ever imagine." Whenever one of the robed men spoke, it always seemed as though their voices joined together and came out of empty space instead of a man's mouth. The acolyte started to hobble towards the podium as the two old men switched places. They nearly fell over as they collided with each other in the center of the room, their blindness almost comical.

"Being surrounded by old blind men in a temple is not how I envisioned my career. Things could certainly be worse, I suppose. I'll be back in a week, however much time that feels like for you who wear the robes." The Major exited the building and headed for his car across the street. Things seemed to be moving along rather well, considering the slight wrench that was thrown into their intricate plans.

Chapter 7

"We can't stay here any longer," Frank said. We all knew he was right. After the distraction with the methane canister we didn't even have a fire. Our trashcan was reduced to shrapnel and debris scattered all over the pavement. The nights were starting to get colder and we needed a place to stay.

"Do you know any other suitable places, Red? Preferably one a bit more out of the way than an abandoned lot on the side of the road." It was only a matter of time before the cops came back in full force with their German shepherds and other nasty tricks. "I remember seeing some abandoned properties from that hill by the chemical lab. They couldn't have been more than a few miles from there."

"I know those places. You're right, except for one thing. That part of town has too much money. Folks around there would notice us and probably report us. We need to stick to the poor sections. Thankfully, whole neighborhoods have been abandoned farther into the *real* ghetto."

"Yeah," Frank chimed in, "ever since the democrats passed all those taxes on the wealthy businessmen, most of them that didn't go bankrupt simply left."

"Wow, I've lived in this city my whole life and never thought about any of that, I always just ignored politics. The way you guys put it I feel like I live in Detroit. All of my high school friends and most of the teachers just voted for anything that the unions said was good." I was glad to be surrounded by people much older and wiser than myself in that moment. "So, which neighborhood do you suggest, Frank?"

"I say we head out, down past 54th street, by the lake and the golf course. No one has lived there in years. The houses aren't that large, but we should be able to simply walk right into one and claim it. Assuming no other homeless guys have already done the same. Ivan, you in?"

"Of course," Ivan said with a smile, "let's do it. I could go for a nice house with some walls to keep the wind out." So it was settled. We were going to claim a house. It took a little over an hour to find the right neighborhood but Frank was right, everything was deserted. We walked down the lane, Forest Berry Avenue, looking for one that seemed devoid of squatters.

"Here, let's try this one. All the windows are still in and it reminds me of the house I grew up in," I said, pointing to a traditional brick house that looked like it was once the perfect suburban stereotype. At my suggestion, we walked up the winding concrete path, now covered in weeds, to the front door. "We ring the doorbell, if no one answers, we find a way in." The doorbell didn't work so Frank pounded on the door. Red was peering through the small slits in the boards covering the first floor windows when the door opened.

"Hey!" Frank yelled out as a grimy hand reached through the opening and pulled him through with surprising strength. It happened so fast that none of us were able to stop the door from closing and locking.

"Move, Red!" I yelled as I grabbed a board from the window and ripped it off with my arm. It didn't take long to get a second board off the window and to shatter the glass. I jumped through the opening, crunching glass beneath my feet, and heard the sounds of Ivan and Red doing the same.

"What do you want?" The voice was shaking, obviously scared. It was a woman, holding Frank hostage. She was covered head to toe in what I hoped was just dirt, holding a broken piece of glass to my friend's throat, a small drop of blood starting to trickle down his skin. Two other women, younger although equally filthy, stood behind the first, one brandishing a club made from old nails and a chair leg, the other wielding a small piece of brass piping. Behind them, in what used to be the house's kitchen, was something altogether frightening.

The tile in the kitchen was torn up and the floor was just a layer of muddy dirt. There was a fire ring of stones in the center of the floor with a spit made out of bits of chair standing over the smoldering coals. Strewn all about the room and heaped into piles in the corners were bones. I didn't have enough time to try to identify them and I wasn't sure that I wanted to. All that was missing from the scene was a bloody pentagram.

"Calm down," I put my hands in the air to try and settle the three deranged women. I could see them in the back of my mind, performing some sort of cruel séance, Frank lying in a pool of blood on the center of a stone altar. I forced the images of human sacrifice out of my mind, I had more pressing issues to resolve. "We don't want to hurt you. Just let our friend go and we will leave your house. We were just looking for somewhere to stay. We didn't know anyone was here. Just let us leave."

"How do we know you aren't here to kill us and eat us?" The one holding the club was obviously insane. It was probably just my imagination, but I thought I saw a bit of spit starting to foam at the edges of her mouth.

"Eat you? What the hell kind of people are you?" Red exclaimed. The piece of glass pushed farther into Frank's neck and he gasped, the blood starting to run quicker.

"Look, needles, they're just junkies," Ivan whispered. It wasn't until then that I noticed all of the used needles around my feet. Sections of rubber tubing littered the floor as well. Frank was starting to look desperate. I winked at him as I turned my head to face Ivan directly. I didn't have to say anything, I just smiled.

Frank, almost reading my mind, was the first one to move. His hands were locked firmly around the forearm of his captor and he yanked down with all of his might while sending his elbow into the fragile face of the much shorter woman. Her soft nose exploded in blood and she fell to the floor. I knew she wasn't physically out of the fight, but mentally, she was done, traumatized by the sudden blow. I sprang to the right side of Frank, leaping to intercept the pipe that was fast approaching the back of his head. I reached my arm out a few inches above Frank's head and took the full force of the club, keeping Frank's brains inside his skull for the moment. The look on the woman's face as she heard the two metal objects collide was beautiful. In the moment she stood there stunned, I retracted my arm and shot it straight out, this time hitting her firmly in the stomach.

She dropped the pipe and doubled over in pain, only to find Frank's fist hitting her with a savage uppercut. I fully expected to see teeth littering the floor from the sound of the punch. The third woman, wielding the tetanus ridden chair leg, had scored a hit on Ivan's shoulder. It didn't look serious but Ivan wasn't a fighter, he was hard pressed. The woman came on him swinging with abandon, her drug fueled rage battering Ivan, forcing him up against the broken window we had just come through. Seeing no other option, I charged her from behind, using the weight of my arm to club the back of her skull. To my surprise, she took the hit in stride and kept on swinging. I grappled her then, using my prosthetic to pin her weapon hand to her chest and my other arm to scoop up her legs and lift her off the ground. She dropped the club and tried to scratch and bite at me, like caged raccoon.

Still holding her a foot or so off the ground, Red stepped forward and punched her square in the jaw. The dirty woman slumped in my arms and I let her fall. We stood there amidst the writhing, strung out druggies, Frank clutching his throat, Ivan holding his shoulder, and Red just standing there staring, bewildered.

"Well, what do we do? Should we just leave them here look for another house?" I had no intentions of staying near these lunatics.

"Don't get ahead of yourself, Esau," Red always came through with the ideas. "This place might actually be perfect.

Think about it. These suburban homes always have a basement. We let the loony crew here occupy the first floor; we can set up shop in the basement and we will never be disturbed. If anyone comes to this place looking for us they won't stay long once they see this lot." He was pointing to the three crazies we had just incapacitated, letting his plan unfold. "It could work. Plus, if we just go on our way and leave them alive, they will tell all of their junkie friends about us. We have enough people on our tail, we don't need some drug dealer or pimp after us for retribution. The only way I see it, we either kill them and leave, or we stay, living in the basement."

Everyone was quiet, except for the occasional groan of pain from the women on the floor. The four of us stood there, contemplating our next move. "Aw man, we can't just kill them all. Look, they probably haven't even eaten in days," Ivan said, sounding sorry for them. "Although judging by the smell, I don't want any part of whatever they cook. My sister and I never had any heart for killing. We have to stay." Everyone seemed to be agreeing with Ivan. It was our only possible course of action.

"Well, let's get these nice ladies cleaned up. Esau, Ivan, fix that window up the best you can, we don't want any curious eyes peeking through the windows at night." Red moved over to the most wounded of our new housemates, the woman Frank had bloodied. The three women said nothing as Red fixed them up, using stray bits of cloth to clean the blood off their bodies. Ivan and I were able to use pipe to hammer the planks back into place over the window. They wouldn't hold for long if someone was determined to get in, but appearances were everything after all.

The first night we spent in the abandoned house was nerve-wracking to say the least. There was no real place to sleep in the basement. It was warmer than being outside with the lack of wind, but the floor was unfinished concrete. We had some extra clothes to throw down to make it more comfortable but nothing good enough to call bedding. The women living above us wouldn't part with any of their own belongings so we had to make do with what little we had.

The women upstairs, who we were convinced were witches, were constantly awake; they were so amped up on drugs they never slept. The three of them were always moving around, always making noise, just constantly on the move. It was unsettling enough to know that we were trying to sleep just one floor below a group of crazed drug addicts, but to constantly hear them? It was horrible. No one slept that first night. After a few hours of restlessness from our entire group, we finally decided to set up a watch schedule. It was as much to protect against outside threats of invasion as to protect against our new house mates. I decided to show the group my recent purchase to set everyone at ease.

"Where in the hell did you get that gun?" Frank was the first one to speak after the silence following my revelation.

"Yeah, and why didn't you use it upstairs?" Ivan was quick to put in, pointing at the revolver.

"I didn't want to kill anyone upstairs," Frank was glowering at me, still holding the wound on his neck. "Look, I got it from a pawn shop, after I ran from the cops that last time." No one seemed to like hearing that.

"You are wanted by the police and you went to a pawn shop to buy a firearm? You must be some kind of extra stupid, boy." It was obvious from his tone, no longer the old and wizened voice I was used to, Red was very angry. "You are going to lead those cops straight to us. You put everyone in danger, bringing that gun in here."

"Red, calm down, I may be young but I'm not that stupid! I knew they would trace the gun if I got it legit. This is a street gun, through and through. I bribed the pawn shop owner to hook me up with a clean street gun. This thing can probably be linked to more than one crime, but there is no way in hell that any cops are going to come in here looking for it." I put the gun away in my jacket to try and calm everyone down. They were acting as though the gun had a tracking chip in it and the police were right outside the door, just about to come in and kill us all.

"You ever think what would happen if that shop keeper is on the take from the cops? He could've been alerted to you, had a picture with your name on it. Those cops could've gone to every business in town with a picture of your pretty self, just waiting for you to make a mistake." Ivan waved his hand my direction, a gesture of dismissal. The plain logic and his worried tone set me back on the defensive. I hadn't thought about that.

"Well, um…" I was at a total loss for words. Ivan was probably right. "I'm sorry. I didn't even think of that. I had some money and I was a little shaken up after the chase. I wanted to be able to protect myself. Those cops almost had me when I climbed the first ledge. The taser leads got stuck in the fabric of my jacket so I didn't get hit, luckily. I just felt helpless, not being able to fire back. I'm sorry." I hung my head, embarrassed. What could I do now? We had the gun, we might as well use it. I didn't want those lunatics upstairs coming down and eating us all as we slept and a gun seemed to be the best deterrent that we had.

"Esau, don't worry too much about it. A gun is a gun. There are so many guns on the street, with so many pawn shop types on the take, probably doesn't matter. If you paid the man, I doubt he will say anything, even if the cops come knocking on his front door." The steadiness had returned to Red's voice once more. His calm demeanor did little to settle the whirlpool of thoughts in my mind. "Chances are, if this pawn shop is taking money from the cops, they are probably just as willing to take money from the likes of you. Don't let it get to you too much, kid.

We overreacted. We should be happy we have a gun now, even if you bought it from a less than advisable source."

"Thanks, Red. I just wanted to help out, that's all." No one said anything to that. They understood that I had made a mistake but they also realized that I couldn't fix it now. Getting rid of the gun didn't seem worth it, especially now that we lived under a certifiable madhouse.

"I'll take the first watch. Here, let me take the gun," Frank said, reaching for the pistol. He took the gun from my hand and tucked it under his belt as he took up his watch post on the stairs. There were two small windows set into the basement walls, up high against the ceiling. Red made sure they were locked and wouldn't budge. "We don't have any sort of alarm to set our schedule. It will just have to be done on the fly. When you are on watch, if you feel like there is no possible way to keep your eyes open any longer, just wake someone else up and get some sleep. See you all in the morning." Most of us managed to get at least a little bit of sleep after we established the watch. Much to our pleasure, no one tried to break in, no one was seen peering in through the dirty windows to look at us, and the women upstairs never seemed interested in coming down to say hello.

I was the last one on watch for the night so I got to admire the sunrise through the dusty windows. There was something very mysterious and comforting about watching the gentle rays of light through that small window. It made me feel like I was in a family again, being surrounded by sleeping people, in a house, watching the sunrise. The cold feel of the pistol grip in my hand and the incessant shouting and moving from up above shattered my dream of humanity. There was another thing from above tickling my senses as I woke up my friends: the most peculiar aroma was wafting down the stairs.

"What is that? Those girls upstairs are cooking breakfast?" Ivan rubbed the grogginess from his eyes.

"That doesn't smell like pancakes. That's meat. We better see what they are up to. I swear, if those lunatics eat people, I'm going to shoot all three of them."

"No you won't, Frank," I said, "I have the gun, remember? I get to shoot them if they eat people, not you." I lead our small troop up the stairs, pistol at the ready, poised to shoot if our housemates turned out to be cannibals. In the center of the kitchen, on the small wooden spit over the cooking fire, was a very interesting sight. Two bats and half of a rabbit were slowly roasting over the fire, grease dripping down to crackle and pop in the flames. "What on earth are you three eating?" I was astounded. Everyone was.

"We have a little bat nest upstairs, in the attic. Every few nights, more bats come in to roost in it. Pretty good tasting bats, too." The oldest looking woman in the group, who seemed to be their leader, didn't look up from her small roasted animal breakfast as she said it.

"I have some traps set up in the woods out back. We catch rabbits there all the time. Usually just little ones though." The trap setter of the group introduced herself as Maria. Her twin sister Mary was sitting across the fire from her, still nursing her wounds from the night before. I was right; the first one to speak was their leader. Her name was Abigail, we soon learned. She was also related to the twins, a sister, but four years older. Mary and Maria were incredibly identical, underneath all of the dirt and grime. They were impossible to tell apart.

Abigail sat there in the dirty kitchen, her long legs tantalizingly set before her. She had striking features, bright green eyes, messy blonde hair cut short and spiked, and she had an air of confidence around her from her years of rugged experience that made her seem mysterious and friendly at the same time. There was a certain pull to her, an intoxicating aura that felt entirely inviting.

"How long have you three been living here?" I asked, trying to take my eyes from Abigail's body. "By the looks of it, you have a pretty efficient set up here, like you've been living this way for years. None of you could be more than thirty years old, by the looks of it. Where is the rest of your family?" Their entire existence was hard to believe.

No longer did I suspect them of witchcraft or even the drug use that was so evident from the needles strewn about the floor. It didn't make sense. The lunatics we had fought with earlier could not have possibly been sane enough to set traps for rabbits and bats and survive.

Abigail responded, "This is our house," she said with a gesture. "We grew up here. Our parents both worked in the big auto factory outside of town on an assembly line. Their jobs got shipped overseas to Japan and we stayed behind to finish school. Remember the tsunami? The whole auto plant was destroyed by the floods and our parents were out of work without enough money to get back to the states. They sent us letters at first, every week. Then the letters only came once a month, then they just stopped altogether. That was about three or four years ago. We just assume they died, they would not have simply forgotten about us." The twins had stopped eating, the story obviously bringing up emotions they didn't want to confront. Abigail brushed a tear from her check before continuing. "So here we are, just living in our house, trying to get by." It was one of the saddest tales I had ever heard. The Red Baron looked like he would cry at any moment.

"And how old are you guys?" I asked, my voice shaking.

"I'm about to turn thirty. The twins are twenty six," Abigail responded, giving me a look that said even though we live together, it goes against social convention to ask a woman her age. "We were able to stay in the house until we finished high school. The bank took it then. They have so many of the houses around here though, they never come to check on them. No one will ever move back into this neighborhood since the whole thing is deserted. There aren't any jobs in the city so we don't have to worry about out of town families looking for houses to buy. In ten years this whole place will be one big ghost town, run by the homeless, until some crime family moves in and takes over. You watch, it'll happen." I stood there, amazed, staring at Abigail. I never knew how bad the city had become.

"Yeah, and when that happens, the three of us will be on top of the whole city. We have our own food source, we stick together, and we know this area better than anyone," the twin named Mary said cheerfully. The woman seemed rather excited for the downfall of the city she grew up in. "Most of the other homeless people living out here in our neighborhood still eat at the soup kitchens and the church missions every day. They moved in here after the neighborhood collapsed, they didn't grow up here. We have the advantage."

We all felt sorry for the three sisters more than anything. The seven of us sat around their dirty fire pit and shared their meal of surprisingly tasty bats and rabbits in silence. No one knew what to say. Any words of encouragement would just be lies. "What do you three do for water here?

Is there a stream in those woods behind the house?" Red asked.

"Here, follow me. I'll show you." We all followed Abigail to the top floor of the house and were astounded by what we saw. There was a small veranda off of the master bedroom, facing the woods behind the house. The three sisters had built a water catchment system on top of the roof with a purification boiler and condenser on the veranda. It was amazing work. Rain water was collected on the top of the roof and then filtered through rubber tubes down into the bathtub which had been ripped up and placed on the balcony. From there, the water traveled through copper tubes where it was heated by fire and then condensed in a metal trash can used to store the purified water. "Sometimes it doesn't rain for a few weeks at a time and we have to ration the water. Luckily, it always snows a lot here so we try to save up extra water in the winter time." She pointed to the closet of the room as she spoke. They had at least thirty or forty plastic jugs filled with water, each holding a gallon.

"How did you three figure this entire thing out? I mean, this is a pretty sophisticated operation. How long did it take to set this up? Who taught you?" Ivan asked, giving a voice to what everyone was thinking. In a way, he was asking 'how did a bunch of young drug addicts develop a working water purification system out of a bathtub and some pipes?' We were all standing there in awe.

"Our dad really wanted to have male children, so when he had three girls and time ran out for our mom to have kids, he became a scout master for a local Boy Scout troop. He was an Eagle Scout himself, and the troop let him take us to the meetings and campouts just for fun. He taught us all about this kind of survival stuff and we liked to learn it. Plus, when he moved with our mom to Japan to work, he left all of his survival books here. We have a whole library of outdoor guides and handbooks and we read them each day. Always prepared, right?" It was amazing; they were three orphaned girls, living in their own house, carrying out their father's dream of having Eagle Scouts for children.

"Talent is worthless unless exercised," Frank mumbled, staring at them in total disbelief. He didn't even realize how offensive his next question was until after he asked it. "But all the needles downstairs, you guys are just homeless drug addicts, how do you do all of this stuff?" Luckily, none of them took offense. Actually, they just started to laugh.

"We aren't drug addicts! Do you see any tracks on our arms? We stole those needles from the junkies that used to live next door. When they died, we cleaned out their place. We leave the needles all around so if anyone looks in or comes through our window," she looked right as me as she said it, a smile widening on her face, "they underestimate us. They think we are just a bunch of heroin addict prostitutes or something and they leave us alone. The plan worked just fine until you guys busted in and nearly killed us." Everyone was laughing out of sheer disbelief by the time Abigail finished with her insane explanation.

Frank smiled as he asked, "You three didn't... eat those junkies when they died... did you?" The girls burst into laughter at that. Clearly, from their setup on the main floor of the house, they appeared to be crazed, cannibalistic junkies when in actuality, they were resourceful, female Boy Scouts with a knack for survival.

"No, silly, of course we didn't *eat* them! They were drug addicts, we probably would've gotten sick from the chemicals poisoning their bodies. We only like to eat the rich folks, nothing tastes as good as plump stock broker or a wealthy investment banker." Abigail could barely keep a straight face as she said it.

"Yeah, and I wouldn't recommend eating any used car salesmen. They taste like greasy fried chicken." The whole notion was preposterous. The twins were laughing so hard they could barely stand and it looked like Red might wet himself at any moment. We had spent an entire night huddled in a cold basement, absorbed by our fear, waiting for someone to come kill us and eat us. It seems that we judged too quickly. No one could have expected this absurd turn of events.

"So, now you guys know everything about us, what's your story? What brought you all here?" We spent the rest of the afternoon explaining everything that had led up to our arrival at their house. None of us were too surprised when our new companions said they wanted to help.

We left the house around midnight, making our way back to the chemical lab to see if we could find some answers. We hadn't really made a plan of action, we just wanted to get in and see if we could figure something out. Any knowledge we could gain would certainly be helpful.

It took a little over an hour to reach Schwartz Laboratories from our house. The guards were still patrolling the area and the gate was closed, just as we expected. "Any ideas on how to get in? We don't want to go in the back way again, it was too weird. We need to break into the main chemical lab," Frank said. "We can drop down the ridge behind the building to get around the fence again."

"I'm betting the twins can distract the guards long enough for someone to sneak into the lab's front door. They probably don't have much staff here at night." Abigail was eager to start our little adventure.

"A place with this kind of security, you know for sure that their front door is going to be locked at all times. We need a way to unlock it without setting off any alarms that will alert the police." Everyone looked to Frank as Red spoke. Frank just shook his head.

"Look at the little black box right next to the door. It's an electronic lock, maybe even a biometric scanner. I can't pick that."

"The twins will go to the guard shack and distract the man inside. I'm guessing there is a button to push inside that shack that will unlock the door from the outside. If not, one of you will have to steal the identification badge from the officer on duty." The twins didn't even say anything, they just walked right up to the guard shack without complaint. Abigail and I got into position to make a bolt for the door.

"Red, you and Frank just run for it if anything goes wrong. No need to get us all caught. We will meet back up at the house." Just as I spoke the words we heard a buzzing noise coming from the door accompanied by the sound of the twins giggling inside the guard shack. Abigail and I ran for the door, pulled it open, and slid inside.

"Welcome to Schwartz Laboratories. How may..." The innocent looking secretary realized we were not where we belonged. I pulled the gun out from my jacket and pointed it straight at the secretary, bringing a finger to my lips, motioning the terrified girl to be quiet.

"Hands in the air!" Abigail yelled. The frightened woman let out a tiny squeak of fright and did as she was told. Abigail moved quickly behind the woman and grabbed a stapler off the desk. She clubbed the secretary so hard in the back of the head

I thought she might have died. The savage blow laid the woman out cold in a split second. "What the hell?" I exclaimed.

"No chances," was all Abigail said as she found a roll of packaging tape in the secretary's desk and used it to tie her up, securing her to the chair.

"Fair enough," I muttered under my breath, wondering if this wasn't the first time Abigail and the twins had broken into a business and tied someone up.

"Esau, start checking the computer, see if there is anything we can learn. I'll make sure no one is coming our way. The place seems dead though." Abigail snuck to the edge of the hallway leading into the lab and took up position as lookout. The computer was opened to a scheduling program. Almost all of the days were blank but I did see the word 'Major' typed into the few spaces.

"Come on, we need to see what they do in this place," I said as I stepped over to where Abigail was crouching and started to move along the corridor. She was right, not many people were working that late at night. We slinked past a couple of doors, none of them having lights turned on or showing any signs of activity. The two of us came to a door that was different than the others. It had the name 'Dr. Matthew J. Kowalski' printed on it in gold. I signaled for Abigail to stop and we waited in front of the closed door, listening. After a few minutes of hearing nothing from inside the office, I reached up and found the door unlocked. We pushed it open, stepped through, and quickly shut it behind us. Abigail found the lights and we both moved to investigate the desk.

"The drawers are all locked," I whispered. "No doubt the computer will be as well." There was one small stack of papers in a wire tray on the desk which Abigail and I both began to read. "Supply order, supply order, supply order... I don't think there is anything good here. I don't know what these chemical names mean anyways." It turned to Abigail to see her standing in front of a bookshelf.

"Look at some of the titles here. *History of the Aum Shinrikyo Cult, Synthesis and Storage of Binary Chemical Compounds, Combating Modern Chemical Terrorism,* Esau, there are tons of books like this. This guy is seriously involved with chemical weapons and, as it seems, terrorism. This can't be good." Abigail was right, this place was heavily involved in at least the study of chemical weapons, if not the production of such agents.

We left the office and continued to sneak down the hallway. At the end of the corridor, past the supply closet I had previously raided, we found the door to the cathedral part of the lab and a second door with a staircase leading down. It was a full six flights of stairs but we eventually made it down to the bottom, only to find the door at the end locked.

"Can you read anything through the window?" Abigail whispered to me as I pressed my face against the small panel of safety glass, her breath hot on my neck.

"Not really. The only thing I can see if a whiteboard and some barrels. Have anything to write with? We should record this." Abigail had a pen in her pocket and wrote down on her hand the chemical compound I read off of the whiteboard: "$C_4H_{10}FO_2P$".

The two of us snuck back to the main lobby of Schwartz Laboratories and found the secretary, tied to her chair, just like we left her. The poor woman was starting to come to her senses as Abigail finished cutting the packaging tape away, setting her free.

"What the… Who are you?" the secretary exclaimed, rightfully fearful. The secretary began to backpedal in her chair, trying to get away from us as fast as possible, lunging for the phone.

Abigail raised her fist up to strike again, "don't make me knock you out twice!" she yelled, making the secretary shriek and raise her arm to meekly defend herself.

"Don't tell anyone we were here." Abigail whispered it into the terrified woman's ear, barely audible. I slowly pulled the revolver out of my pocket, making sure that the woman got a good look at it before sliding it back into my jacket.

For a brief moment, the woman simply did nothing. She just looked at us, crying, and said nothing. Abigail slapped her hard enough to knock the blank stare off of her face.

"Alright, alright! I won't tell anyone, I swear! Just leave me alone, I have a child," the woman pleaded, devoid of any will to resist. Abigail, still leaning close to the woman, grabbed a handful of her hair from the back of her head and ripped it back. The secretary jerked, her hands reaching out for the desk to keep from tipping over.

"Good," was all I heard Abigail say before we left the building and started heading for home. The image of Abigail so ruthlessly terrorizing the poor woman stuck with me the entire walk. Having just met her, I did not think she had the capacity for such violence against an innocent bystander. Living on the street has its price.

Chapter 8

The two of us met up with the others back at the house. "Find anything useful in there?" Red was quick to ask.

"Not as much as we would've liked, but we got enough. I know that the cop, the Major, he is behind or at least involved in all this," I responded.

"We went into someone's office, probably their leader since we didn't see any other offices with names on them. Does the name Dr. Matthew Kowalski ring any bells?" Abigail asked. No one knew anything about him.

"Well, what did you learn?" Red asked, getting impatient.

"This lab is making chemical weapons. We know that for sure. I don't know why, or how that is related to what happened in Vatican City, but they are heavily involved in chemical weapons beyond a doubt," I replied, a grim expression on my face.

"Any idea what kind of chemicals they are working with?" Ivan seemed nervous.

"Yeah, I read a compound name off of a board behind a locked door, probably to the main lab areas. It was pretty deep underground, I'm guessing that its part of their new addition. I don't know what the compound means though, never was any good at chemistry." All eyes turned to Abigail then as she pulled forth a small book from her pocket. It fit in the palm of her hand and was titled *Roger's Field Guide to Chemical Compounds*. "How the hell did you come by that?" I exclaimed, sheer surprise in my voice.

"Swiped it from that guy's library. I'm basically a Boy Scout, remember? Always prepared, always resourceful." Abigail said with a smile. It took a few minutes to find the right section to look up our mystery compound but when we found it, we all understood the implications. They were making sarin gas, one of the world's most deadly chemical nerve agents.

"So, do you think it was sarin gas that killed all those people at the Vatican?" Red asked, more somber than I had ever seen him.

"No, I don't think it could've been. I wouldn't have lived through it for one. And I don't think a gas attack could cause that kind of widespread death so quickly. Anyways, I felt a vibration when it happened. A gas attack wouldn't do that." What on Earth could have done it? I was still no closer to an answer.

"So, they aren't using the gas to kill people, at least not yet. Why would they need to make it? Judging from the amount of barrels that Esau and I saw in that room, they have a decent amount of the stuff. Probably enough to kill most of what is left of this poor city." Abigail sounded just as frightened as we all did. A long moment passed before anyone spoke again. We were all just thinking about what it all meant, how many more people could die if they attacked another city with the deadly nerve agent.

"The only thing we know for sure is that this 'Major' guy wants you dead, Esau. We have to get some insurance. I can't imagine that the entire police force is in on it too. The Major is probably just using the regular officers as pawns. We need to get some sort of evidence so that if you do get captured, you can at least try to blow this whole thing open. If they take you now, they will probably just hand you over to the Major without hesitation. Without any hard evidence, your story is too preposterous to believe."

"You're right, Frank. We need insurance. Not just to protect my own skin, but you guys too. Who knows how many people they are willing to kill to keep their secret." I shuddered at the thought of my friends dying to protect me.

"I think we know the answer to that question…" Tears started to roll down Ivan's face. Of course they would kill our entire group if we were taken alive. They already killed Sarah, as far as we knew. Why would they hesitate to kill again? Perhaps the police officers themselves wouldn't pull the trigger but either way, we would all die.

"Twins, why don't you two go get us some food for tonight. And you won't have to sleep in the basement anymore. We are either all in this together, or not at all. The three of us want to help you. To tell you the truth, we welcome a bit of adventure, even if it does put our lives in jeopardy. Living in this old house, even if we may have food and water, will kill us all eventually. We have nothing to do, no purpose. Building our supplies and setting our traps out in the woods kept our minds occupied long enough, but now we need a purpose. I think your dilemma may have saved the three of us from insanity." Abigail was smiling as she spoke, true sincerity in her voice.

"Let me talk to my friend down on Vine Street, he might have some ideas for us and some supplies. If we are going to try to bust this whole thing open, I'm sure some recording equipment might help. Heck, he might even already know something useful. If anyone in the ghetto knows anything, it's him." Red turned his smile of confidence to me, asking with his body language for my approval.

"Sounds like a plan. I'll go with you in the morning," I said, returning his smile.

"Wait, this isn't Dime is it? That hot shot prison rat covered in tattoos?" Frank asked, more than a little concerned.

"The very same. Mr. Dime. I'm still not sure why you distrust such a fine and upstanding citizen, Frank. In all of my dealings with him he has been nothing but the utmost gentleman," Red replied with a smile.

"Why do they call him 'Dime'?" I asked, confused by the exchange.

"Everyone says his name is Jericho del Armgo, but people just call him Dime now. He did ten years in prison for killing ten men. He has a thing with tens so he earned the nickname Dime," Red explained.

"Wait, you are telling me that this guy killed ten men and only served a decade in prison? He should have been executed." It was absurd to think that such a heinous crime could go so lightly punished.

"Well, see now, as the story goes, when young Jericho was just fifteen years old, a gang of drug dealers and pimps, general lowlifes, broke into his house at night. Ten of them. They raped his mom and stabbed her to death. Jericho hid in a linen closet through the whole thing. Thinking they were alone in the house, the ten attackers helped themselves to the liquor cabinet. They all passed out or fell asleep drunk after not too long. Young Jericho came out of his linen closet, saw them sleeping there, drunk in his own house, the body of his dead mother on the floor, and he went into the kitchen and got himself a knife. Jericho cut the head off of every single man in that house that night." My mouth fell open as Red told the story.

"Oh my God…" I could barely believe it.

"Don't stop there, Red," Frank interjected. "Tell him the rest of the story, the best part."

"Well see, the law won't send a man to prison for a decade for killing his own mother's attackers in his own house, even if they were passed out and defenseless. What sent Jericho to the highest security prison in the state was what the police found the next day when Jericho reported the break in," Red continued.

"I'm not even sure I want to hear this. I can't imagine what that kid went through," I managed to say.

"As it turns out, Jericho was busy the whole night. He had dug a small pit in the back yard behind his house. He dragged all ten of those headless bodies out to the pit and doused them in gasoline."

"Oh come on, Red, tell him the good part! No one cares that he burned the bodies, tell him about the heads!" Frank was bubbling with excitement by this point in the story.

"Alright, fine. As you can imagine," Red continued, "Jericho burned the bodies and buried their ashes in the pit. What he did with the heads, well, the police and the paramedics that arrived at the scene still don't talk about it. The authorities found fifteen year old Jericho asleep under a blanket on his front lawn around noon the next day. Behind him, partially blocked by some landscaping, was a wooden fence post, freshly driven into the ground. Jericho had taken a roll of duct tape and taped every single head to the sides of that pole. All the heads were looking up to the sky and they had pennies over their eyes." The gruesome story almost made me sick as it brought images of all those corpses filling Saint Peter's Square.

"Tell him about the sign! You can't leave out the sign," Fred exclaimed.

"On the top of the pole was a cardboard sign that Jericho had made. The official police report never said what he used for paint, but by all accounts it was as thick and red as human blood."

"What did it say?" I dared to ask.

"Written in blood for all to see, it read: The Last Argument of Kings." Red finished his gruesome tale with a smile.

Frank was practically giddy by the end of the story. It was obvious that this man, Jericho del Armgo, was as much of a folk legend with the homeless as the Red Baron himself. "The judge, when he sentenced Dime, asked him why he did it. Dime only said that if he did anything less than butcher the men who attacked his family, he would have lost his honor along with his mother that night. He asked the judge to give him the time. They were going to just send him to juvenile hall until he was eighteen, but Dime asked for ten years of hard time, with the general population. The judge gave it to him! Dime told the whole courtroom that he was proud of what he had done and that he wanted to spend a year in prison to remember each life he justly ended."

"I can't wait to meet this hero in the flesh tomorrow," I said. Much to my surprise, Frank was clearly against the idea.

"I wouldn't go meet with him if I were you. Rumor has it he kills anyone who speaks to him wrong or looks at him funny. He cuts your head off right in the middle of the street if he doesn't like you." Red and I both started to laugh, it was just a rumor after all.

"Frank, you need to calm down. I've dealt with Dime for a few years now, never had any trouble," Red chuckled as he spoke, "it's true, he killed those ten men fourteen years ago, but I would bet my life he hasn't killed a man since. What Dime did, he did to preserve his honor and earn his manhood. Can't argue with that. He has nothing left to prove to anyone. He has the world's respect already." Red was right, as usual. After what Dime had done, it would be difficult to expect anything other than complete pacifism from him.

We left the house at the break of dawn to go find Dime the next morning. According to Red, Dime always stayed around a particular used book store in the heart of the ghetto. We found him there, two hours after sunrise, sitting in an old wicker chair in front of the store, reading a book. He looked much like any hardened felon would. He was wearing dirty leather boots, torn jeans, and a dusty denim jacket that looked like it used to belong to a motorcycle gang member.

Just as Frank had said, Dime was covered head to toe in tattoos. His head was shaved and even his scalp had ink. It was hard to tell what that tattoos depicted but they had a kind of flowing motion to them that it appeared as though it was all part of the same design. His arms, what little was showing from under the denim jacket, were covered in tree branch designs. The sides of his wrists had leaves, some falling, but most attached to the branches that ran down his arms. His head was similarly tattooed with branches, but they were all barren. It was as though his arms and hands displayed autumn while his neck and head were winter. There was something oddly captivating about Dime. He looked so peaceful, sitting in front of a book store and reading. Dime gave off the feeling as if he had spent an entire lifetime in that chair and intended to spend another lifetime in the same fashion. If it weren't for the horribly graphic story I had recently heard from Dime's past, I would have expected him to be some sort enlightened philosopher, perhaps even the store's owner.

"Well, well, look who it is, my old friend Red. Good to see you, man," even for this early in the morning, Dime was as cheerful as can be, happy enough to see Red that he stood up and gave him a hug right there. When he put his book down on the small coffee table next to his chair I couldn't help but glance at the title. I was amazed to see a copy of *The Aeneid* resting on that table. The book was worn and its spine was cracked a thousand times.

Dime let Red out of his embrace and looked to me, smiling. "*The Aeneid*, a classic," I said, nodding towards his book.

"Yes, well, when I'm not helping this old man in some epic journey or another, I like to let my mind wander. What better place for it to end up than in the arms of one as beautiful as Queen Dido." They way he spoke shattered his entire image and ruined the whole story of his childhood I had heard earlier. The words flowed from his mouth like a college professor giving a lecture over his favorite work, a lecture he had given hundreds of times before and knew by heart. The contrast of Dime's background, appearance, and obvious intelligence was perplexing to say the least, even disconcerting and unsettling.

"Well then, good sir, I mourn your loss. To know that such a fine woman as the Queen of Carthage would kill herself must be troublesome," I said as I shook the man's hand. I knew I had caught him off guard in the best possible way.

"Yes, but is it not better to have loved one such as Dido than to have given your heart to, say, Andromache perhaps, only to know that she would later father another man's children in her slavery? Dido may not have made a *perfect* wife, but the world has only ever been large enough to contain one Penelope." The tattooed philosopher said is wistfully, as if remembering the great women of antiquity from his own personal experiences.

"Dime, we came here to inquire about some potential resources. Is there somewhere we can talk?" With a wave of his hand, Dime led us into the bookstore and to a small room at the back of the building. The bookstore was incredibly cluttered with old tomes in dusty jackets. The bookshelf along the entire back wall was only half as tall as the other bookshelves in the store. It had white plaster busts of famous authors and philosophers resting atop it. Walking to the back of that bookstore felt like walking through a pantheon of literary gods.

Dime set his copy of *The Aeneid* on the top of that half sized bookshelf, leaning it between a bust of Virgil and the stony white likeness of Montesquieu.

After fiddling with a massive key ring for a few moments before finding the right key, Dime opened the door at the back of the bookstore. The room was dark, dusty, and smelled strongly of mold. There was a single light bulb hung from a cord in the center of the room. The globe was so covered in dust that the light barely illuminated anything in the small room. The pieces of furniture in the area were two small three-legged wooden stools and a couch that was passable as being from *The Titanic*.

Dime took his place on the center of the couch and motioned for us to sit across from him on the stools. The space was so small that it took a conscious effort for everyone's knees to avoid awkwardly bumping in the middle. Red shut the door behind us and the meeting began.

"So, the word is on the street that you two are in some nasty trouble together," Dime began. "The cops have been by here a few times already, asking about you, kid. They have a picture of you, too. Don't worry too much about it though, no one in the ghetto ever helps the cops. Most of us here are convicts in one way or another so there are very few rats to be found." That was reassuring. The cops were still after me in full force but at least this part of the city was rallying around me. Or at least everyone hated the police enough to hide me. Either way, it was welcome news.

"We need your help," Red began. "Esau has stumbled into a huge government conspiracy, one of the largest cover up operations I have ever heard of. He was just at the wrong place at the wrong time. We need to figure out a way to expose this thing."

"Surveillance equipment, then. You want cameras, mini recorders, that kind of thing? Do you know where to start?" Dime asked, hardly believing that Red and I were up to the task.

"We've broken into their operation twice now. We need to either record them speaking in there or a better way to steal enough evidence to prove our case." That seemed to impress Dime. He leaned forward on his old couch and looked right at us.

"If you do this, if you really want to pull this off without any hitches, I need to know something. The authorities say you are wanted for murder, kid. They have the word 'terrorist' written under your photograph. Did you do anything to earn that label?"

"I can promise you that I have never had anything to do with any sort of terrorist group and I have never killed anyone. What happened-" Dime cut me off.

"No details. I trust you on your word. I don't want to know what happened, just that you deserve my help. I've known the Red Baron here long enough to know that when he vouches for someone, I should too." Dime relaxed back into his couch with a smile on his face. We had passed his test.

"Here is what I can do for you," Dime continued, "the cops think they have me turned. That puts me in a unique position for misinformation. Tell me where you two are living and I will lead them astray. Tell me which government building you plan on hitting and I can make sure they are looking in the wrong direction when it goes down. I can get your equipment too, no worries there."

"That sounds like just what we need, Dime," Red said in all seriousness. "Two or three small sound recorders should be enough to get our information." Red told him about the house we were living in and set up the plan for complete misdirection. It was all coming together nicely.

Red nodded to me and I took what little money I had, totaling $210, and put it on the table. Dime looked down at the crumpled pile of bills for a long while before scooping them up in his hands. He counted out the bills and sighed. "You know this won't get you much. These kinds of operations are the most risky kind. You should have come in here with triple this," Dime said quietly.

"I'm sorry," I said, "it's all I have left."

"I know. I assumed as much. That's why I'm only going to take a hundred. You need this more than I do, that much is easy to tell." Dime handed over the remaining bills and put them directly into my hand. I was astonished to say the least. "I like you, kid," he continued, "and Red, you know I owe you this much and more. If all of this works itself out, consider our debts even. I'll be in it with you until the end."

I put the money back into my pocket and stood up in the cramped space to leave. Dime remained seated as we left the small meeting room. "Two days," he called out behind us, "Godspeed."

"So," I remarked as we exited the bookstore into the morning sunlight, "you two have a history together it would seem." Red just nodded and smiled and continued down the sidewalk in the direction of our house.

Chapter 9

"So," Abigail said later that night, after we had finished our greasy meal of roasted bats and rabbits, "what's your story, Esau? I mean, you seem pretty smart, shouldn't you be in college right now, getting drunk every night and sleeping through classes?" Everyone chuckled, looking at me expectantly.

"Well," I began, not sure I wanted to tell them much about my history. Even with my closest friends, I was always pretty private, keeping to myself whenever possible. I decided that lying would be easier than telling them what had happened, for my sake. "My parents were both in the military," it seemed plausible enough, "they were deployed to Afghanistan when the war broke out, my mom was in the Air Force and my dad was in logistics with the Navy. I lived with my brother for a while, until he got a job offer and moved away. I have an apartment to myself now and I was planning on going to college next year." I shook my head, "doesn't seem likely now."

"Are your parents still deployed? Did they ever make it back?" Red asked, a concerned expression stamped on his wrinkled face.

"They are still there, in Afghanistan I mean," it was hard to lie to them, knowing they cared about me, "well, my mom was captured when her helicopter went down, they never found her. From what the government told me, my dad went after her, they didn't find him either." Red patted me on the back, trying to show support.

"That's pretty rough, man," Ivan said, the others nodding their agreement.

"Yeah, I responded, "it's not as bad as it sounds. I was never really close to them to begin with. They weren't home that often and my brother is ten years older than me so he raised me anyways." That part was true at least, very true. "What about you, Red? Care to tell us how you got those medals on your hat?" Luckily, my diversion worked. Red was more than eager to tell us the story of his war heroics and all the lives he saved.

The seven of us stayed up late into the night, Red telling war stories, Ivan and Frank yelling about conspiracy theories and politics. Things seemed to be looking up for us, with Dime getting supplies and working his magic with the police.

We woke up early the next morning to the sound of fists pounding on the back wall of the house. The twins were grabbing their weapons and preparing a defense by the time Red got a chance to look out a window and identify the source of the commotion. Dime had to enter through the front door as it was the only still working portal into the ramshackle house.

"I think I have everything you need, can't stay for breakfast though," Dime said, looking down at the half of a rabbit still smoking on the spit from the night before, "I have other pressing engagements to attend. Do enjoy your lovely meal," he remarked, shaking his head at the sight of our kitchen.

"Thanks, Dime. This stuff means a lot. I owe you, man," I said, waving as Dime walked out the door.

"No you don't," he called over his shoulder, "I did this one for Red, not for you." With that, Dime was gone. The supplies had been delivered in an old fashioned satchel made from heavy brown paper and twine, like a package of ground beef bought from a butcher shop in the Great Depression. It was peculiar packaging, and probably difficult for a homeless man to produce. I didn't mention the extra effort it must have taken Dime to make our resources look presentable, albeit antiqued. I assumed it had at least something to do with the past relationship between Dime and Red, but if Red wanted to tell us all about it, he would have by now, so I let it go.

That brown paper package had a good deal more than the sound recorders we requested. The first thing my eyes, and inevitably my hands, went to was a small metal case that could easily pass for a fancy cigarette holder from the era of mobsters and prohibition. I opened the case slowly, not sure what to expect. The little metal cigarette holder was filled with four tiny syringes, each one about half filled with a thin red liquid. "What on earth are these?" I asked, holding up the syringes for everyone to see.

"Let me take a look," Ivan said, taking the case from my hand. "Here, behind the needles is a note. It says 'Sweet Dreams: half shot, drowsy and confused, full shot, sleep, two shots, morgue.' Wow. This stuff could definitely come in handy." Ivan smiled, obviously intrigued by our new toys.

The rest of the package was full of more surprises. The two small sound recorders were there, just as we had requested, along with a compact handheld device to play back the memory from the recorders. The recorders themselves were black, about the size of a quarter, with a very sticky adhesive on one side and a small plastic pull tab sticking out from one side with the label '24h' printed on it.

All told we had three digital watches, four vials of sweet dreams, two voice recorders, the playback device, a small but very powerful flashlight, and a compact gas mask that fit snugly over just the mouth and nose. "I say we came out pretty well in this deal. Now, when do we go in again for the evidence? The sooner we go, the better, as I'm sure you guys understand," I said, admiring our loot and trying to formulate a plan.

"We should try tonight," Frank said, "I don't like just waiting around here for them to make the next move. If we can get some real evidence of what they're doing in there and take it to the media, we might be able to bring their whole operation down." Everyone nodded in agreement, we had to act quickly.

"Maria, Mary, you two take one of the watches, you two always stick together anyways. Abigail, you and Esau can keep one of the watches also. The third will stay with Red, Ivan, and myself. Sound fair?" Frank asked. Everyone nodded.

"That should work. Looks like the watches are already synchronized. Perfect," I said. We divided the rest of the supplies among us. The playback device was kept in the house and Abigail claimed the gasmask for herself. We didn't really know what to do with it, or even if it would help against the sarin gas, should that become an issue, but Abigail seemed intent on keeping it for herself and since no one had any better ideas for it, we just let her have it.

She tried on the small gas mask, making sure it fit. Something about her dirty, bedraggled appearance behind the mask was oddly attractive, in a very cyberpunk, futuristic kind of way. I imagined her going to a techno rave, or some other intense concert, ready to party. We weren't going to a concert though, we were going to risk our lives to expose a government plot and hopefully rescue our friend Sarah from the clutches of an evil mastermind. I had bigger things to worry about than how a woman twelve years my senior looked in a gas mask. Thankfully, for my sake, Abigail removed the mask as quickly as she had put it on.

We were busily brainstorming ideas for how to best get enough information on the sound recorder to protect us when we heard the sounds of boots running on the concrete outside our house. Everyone stopped talking and went quiet, looking at the door, expecting it to come crashing it at the end of a battering ram. Abigail began to slowly strap the gas mask onto her face as we gathered up the rest of the supplies and everyone started to head for the basement door. We heard numerous shouts outside and saw the flashing of police lights coming through the cracks and gaps in the boards covering the windows.

"Wait," Frank said as one of the twins opened the basement door, "I don't think they are coming for us, they would've been in by now," he whispered, frightened.

"Girls, get downstairs and hide, stay quiet. Red, you and Ivan go with them, if they come in here they will want Esau, if we give him up, they won't even bother to look in the basement." Abigail was motioning for the twins to continue down the steps into the basement and they obeyed. I didn't like the idea of not trying to hide, but if it saved everyone else, it was a necessary risk. "Follow me," Abigail whispered from behind the gas mask to Frank and I as we followed Abigail up the steps to the top floor.

She led us to an empty bedroom with a large window facing the street. Nothing was covering the window so we had to creep up to it from the side and cautiously peer around the edge of the frame to look out. Abigail looked first. She turned back to us with an expression in her eyes not of fear, but relaxed and calm. "They are at the wrong house! They aren't here for us. It's ok." She took the mask off and slipped it into a pocket, clearly not worried about our plight any longer.

I couldn't believe it. I scrambled in front of Abigail and looked out the window to see four police cars and a large black town car arrayed in front of the house across the street. Armored police officers were moving all around the house, guns trained on the windows and doors. The three of us stood there in the bedroom, still afraid but no longer fearing for our own lives, and watched as they brought a heavy black ram up to shatter the front door. The first hit seemed to make such a loud noise that it shook the whole neighborhood. On the second hit, the door exploded into a thousand splinters of old wood. When the dust cleared, it seemed as though the door never existed in the first place.

Half a dozen police officers charged through to the broken door, a riot shield leading the way. We heard a gunshot followed by confused and incomprehensible yelling, and then there was a pause. Was it over? We heard a second gunshot, this time much louder. The second shot must have come from one of the shotguns a few of the officers were carrying. I grimaced as I looked at Abigail, knowing what was happening in that house and knowing that it was meant for us.

"Did you know the people that lived in that house?" I asked her, my voice trembling. Abigail wrapped her arms around my waist and buried her head in my chest. I felt a violent shake run through her body knew at once that she had indeed known them. "Frank, head to the basement and tell everyone that it's over, the cops went to the wrong house." I motioned with my free hand to the door and Frank got the message, giving Abigail some privacy.

As soon as we were alone I could feel Abigail start to cry, her tears wetting my shirt. I held her in as warm a hug as I could give and just stood there in the window with her as an ambulance arrived on the scene across the street. She turned her head, still pressed firmly against my chest, to look out the window. We both just stared in disbelief as officers milled about the yard in front of the house, seemingly at ease. The paramedics got out of their ambulance and weren't in any sort of hurry. We could see them joking with some of the officers, lackadaisically bringing supplies and a stretcher out of the back of the ambulance.

Abigail was sobbing into my shirt, trying not to break down and weep openly. The paramedics went into the house pushing their stretcher and supplies before them. "Everything will be ok, Abigail," I didn't know what to say to comfort her. I couldn't be sure if it was the brutal display of force used against people she knew that had so moved her or if it was simply the fact that we knew it was meant for us that caused her to cry. "Just let it out, trying not to cry will only make it hurt more," I managed to whisper past the lump forming in my own throat.

A moment later the paramedics came back out of the house, a body on the stretcher they were pushing between them. Even though the corpse was covered by a white sheet, the blood was beginning to show through. Abigail burst fully into tears at the gruesome sight. The way that the authorities were treating the entire situation was what bothered my heart the most. As I stood there, trying to be strong for an emotionally wounded friend, I couldn't help but stare in amazement at the callous disrespect the police officers were displaying.

Most of the policemen were leaning against the sides of their cruisers, talking, acting as though nothing out of the ordinary had happened. One officer went over and lifted the cover off of the body to briefly glance at the carnage. Just when I was about to think that at least one of the brutes had an ounce of compassion I saw him turn to his fellow officers, smiling. A couple of them clapped him on the back and one even shook his hand. What I had hoped with all my heart to be a shred of human decency and respect was actually just the shooting officer inspecting his work and gloating over the kill. The man was acting like a hunter, considering whether or not the deer he just downed was large enough to mount.

A man in a suit emerged then from the house, a man I instantly recognized as the Major, an old pearl-handled revolver strapped to his side. I pulled Abigail, still clinging to me, out from view of the window and rolled to my side against wall of the house. As I spun the two of us out of the Major's view, my foot got caught up on a piece of torn carpet and we tumbled to the floor. My back thudded painfully into the hard carpet, absorbing all of the force. "What is it?" Abigail asked, barely loud enough to be audible.

"The Major, he was there. They were definitely after me. They just had the wrong house," I whispered back. That seemed to bring even more tears to Abigail's eyes. We laid there on the dirty carpet for a few moments, neither of us saying anything, while she calmed down and her crying subsided. My shirt was thoroughly wet with her salty tears when she finally stopped shaking.

I lifted her up above my chest a few inches and looked at her face, red with tears. "Are you going to be alright?" I asked. She nodded and wiped a line of tears from her face with the back of her hand. I leaned up, attempting to stand her up and shake the dust from my back but Abigail didn't move. She simply held her position, straddled over my legs. As I began to rise, our faces were just millimeters apart. She kissed me then, gently on the lips, for just a short moment. The kiss caught me completely off guard, instantly pushing all thoughts of the murder I had just witnessed from my mind. I pulled back from the kiss and she stood up, reaching a hand down to lift me from the floor.

"Um, Abigail," I stammered, "You are almost double my age…" I didn't know what to say but as soon as I said that, I knew it was the wrong thing to say. Actually, it wasn't just the wrong thing to say, it was probably the worst thing I could have said. If Abigail was offended, which she certainly had to be, she did a good job hiding it.

"Just…" She was equally confused by the situation. "Don't say anything. Think of it as a thank you for comforting me." With that she turned and walked out of the room, back down the stairs.

"You could have just said it then," I mumbled in disbelief, knowing she couldn't hear me. Even as the words passed my lips, a smile broke out on my face.

Downstairs, everyone was pretty shaken. Abigail told the story of the murder we had just watched, pointedly leaving out the part where our lips had met. As it turns out, the man who had been living in the abandoned house had been somewhat of a mentor to the three women. When the neighborhood was first abandoned, the man, in his early years of retirement, had brought food to the sisters on a regular basis. They didn't know him personally, but he represented kindness. Abigail had just watched the first person other than her parents who had ever shown her kindness get brutally murdered by the police. She didn't openly cry while she told the story but it was clear to everyone that she was struggling to hold the tears back.

The twins, who didn't know the man as well, were not nearly as moved by the killing as their older sister. "So, Esau," Maria asked, "do you think that if they find you, they will just shoot you and take your body away like that man?" It was a good question, one I didn't want to think about.

"I'm not sure. I know they want me dead but I don't know if they would just shoot me on sight or not. I like to think that they would take me to the police station at least. I have no doubts that if I am ever captured, I will have less than seventy two hours to live, but I still hold hope that my life would continue for at least a day after my surrender." It was the best answer I could give, the best honest answer at least. No one said anything for a long time.

"One thing is for sure, we need to get some sort of evidence. Even if it can't save you if you are taken alive, it will at least give us the hope that maybe we can figure out whatever is going on here and bring an end to it." Everyone nodded their agreement with Red. We had to do something. After the display of force across the street, we all knew that our time was running dangerously low. Even if we all died, bringing an end to whatever evil was at work here would be reward enough, and hopefully bring some closure to the fallen victims at Vatican City.

"What do we do?" I asked, eager to make a plan.

"We need to get the recorder planted on someone inside the laboratory, preferably that Dr. Kowalski person. He seems to run the show. Mary, Maria, do you girls think you can handle it?" Abigail had composed herself enough to start organizing our makeshift task force, donning her aura of command like an old pair of comfortable shoes.

"We can get it done," Mary said without a hint of fear or hesitation. Everyone was ready to finally do something and feel useful.

"Good. Remember, we also have to retrieve the recorders. These won't transmit wirelessly, only manually," Abigail reminded everyone.

"Let me handle that part," Ivan said, a bit of his old Russian accent starting to break through in his excitement.

"Perfect," Abigail smiled, "We need to get to the lab before Dr. Kowalski does to plant the recorder. Red, being the oldest and therefore the least agile, no offense," Red shook his head, clearly not offended by the remark to his age, "you get to play lookout. I want you on the ridge overlooking the lab, ready to warn us if anything unusual happens. Deal?"

"Certainly," Red replied with a smile, happy to be away from the dangerous action.

"Good. Frank, you are with Red. Esau, you and I will go out and scout. Any extra information we can glean will certainly help. Ivan, you just, do... whatever it is you plan on doing. Are we all in agreement?" Abigail truly enjoyed the role of the leader. She sounded like a seasoned veteran giving orders to her most trusted troops. Maybe it was her newly discovered assertiveness and drive, or perhaps it was the awkward albeit brief kiss we shared upstairs, but regardless of the reason, I found that all I could think about was us scouting together. My teenage mind told me that there must be some hidden reason for her to assign the two of us on a mission together, alone.

The way she smiled when she spoke, the way she looked each of us in the eye when she gave her orders, the calm manner in which everyone accepted her ideas with nothing but unabashed obedience, it was all intoxicating. For the first time since all of this had started I actually felt like I held some sort of advantage over the Major. I hoped, in my now optimistic mind, that we could and were about to figure this whole thing out.

We waited in the house until an hour or so after midnight, not sure how early Dr. Kowalski would arrive for work. Walking to the laboratory in silence set the tone for the entire adventure. We felt like a military platoon heading deep into enemy territory on a dangerous mission, our fearless leader Abigail walking point. The cool night air only added to the excitement. In my mind, I imagined that we were some sort of armored column, walking down a dirt road between two rice paddies, deep inside North Vietnam. It was a much better image than what we actually were, a smelly band of ragged homeless people walking down the street.

There was a parking garage across from the laboratory with a good view of the entrance. We established our base camp behind a rusty red minivan on the second floor of the garage. "If anything goes wrong, we meet back at the house at ten. If, for any reason, the house becomes compromised, we meet at Dime's bookstore by noon and wait for everyone there. If you aren't there by midnight, we will assume that you have been lost." Our fearless leader had spoken and there was no argument from the soldiers.

"Don't expect me until after Kowalski gets off work and leaves for the night," Ivan put in, not wanting us to leave him behind.

Frank and Red left to make their way to the ridge behind the lab, in perfect view of the building and of the rest of the group. The twins, Abigail, Ivan, and I stayed behind the minivan, watching the laboratory for any signs of action. "The sun is on the rise. The time has come to get into position, girls." At Abigail's command, Mary and Maria stood up and made their way to the ground floor, one on each side of the garage, waiting for Dr. Kowalski to arrive. They each held a sound recorder, ready to place it on the target.

Ivan had dozed off against the small concrete wall of the second floor. With the old Russian asleep, I couldn't help but find myself staring at Abigail. In the soft glow of the parking garage lights, mixing with the advent of dawn, she looked beautiful. Rugged and likely suffering from malnutrition, but she still looked beautiful nonetheless. The air of command about her seemed incredibly fitting, like leadership was meant for her shoulders. Knowing that she had thought up our entire plan only served to make her even more attractive. She caught me glancing her way more than once but she only smiled as I quickly diverted my eyes.

A half an hour or so after sunrise, a nice luxury car driven by a man wearing a lab coat over a suit and tie pulled into the parking garage. It wasn't until then that we realized our dilemma. None of us knew what Dr. Kowalski even looked like. Our best bet was a middle aged scientist of Polish decent.

"Do you think that's our man?" I asked, pointing to the car as it approached.

"It has to be," Abigail responded with confidence. She signaled to the twins and pointed toward the car as it entered the first floor of the garage. The man stepped out, not particularly Polish in appearance, whatever that might look like, and made his way toward the laboratory entrance with a nice leather briefcase dangling by his side.

One of the twins, it was difficult to tell which from a distance, was sitting on the sidewalk near the entrance to Schwartz Laboratories. Instead of her winter coat, she was wearing just a thin windbreaker and a pair of skimpy shorts, looking seductively like a prostitute. Dr. Kowalski was roughly thirty feet from the sidewalk where the woman sat as he noticed her. She let the loose windbreaker slip tantalizingly off one of her shoulders and she tilted her head down, looking at the man, while she slowly replaced it. At that exact moment the other twin, whoever it was, walked up from behind Dr. Kowalski wearing the exact same outfit and brushed into him, causing him to turn.

Her hand went up under the lapel of the older man's jacket as the twin whispered something into Dr. Kowalski's ear and kept walking. The older man simply stood there for a moment, dumbfounded, as he realized that the woman who had bumped into him had been an exact copy of the attractive woman sitting on the curb.

As the walking twin passed by her sister she reached down, took her twin's outstretched hand, and they walked down the sidewalk, hand in hand until they were out of view. It was flawless. Regardless of what Dr. Kowalski might have suspected, he knew nothing of what had just happened. As long as the adhesive on the recorder held and the device functioned properly, we would get what we came for. I smiled at Abigail when the twins were out of sight.

"We couldn't have done it better ourselves," I said, obviously pleased that the operation had gone off without a hitch. I rustled Ivan from his sleep. "Everything is in place. The recorder should be hidden underneath the lapel of the man's overcoat. I'll meet you back at the house." Frank nodded his assent and returned to his dreams.

Abigail and I walked back to the house without speaking much. The air was awkward between us to say the least, the tension palpable. "So, is that a strategy the twins have employed before? They seemed to make it work perfectly," I managed to ask, breaking the silence as we entered the house.

"I can assure you, I had no idea what the twins were planning and I don't think they have ever done that before. When I ask them if they can do something and they say yes, I never doubt them. Those two have always been the resourceful and quick thinking ones of the group," she replied casually.

"Hey, it was all your master plan in the first place, don't sell yourself short of the credit," I said, awkwardly patting Abigail's shoulder.

"Yeah, I hear you, but really, all I had to do was inspire everyone and make them believe we could do it and they came up with the plans themselves," she said, moving out of my reach.

We spent the next hour sitting around the fire pit in the center of the kitchen, waiting for everyone to arrive, silently hoping that everything went well. The twins were the first to come home. "Hey, amazing work. It went off beautifully," I said, offering a high five to each of the girls.

"Yeah, you two did really great. The poor old man was probably so confused and distracted you could've stolen the clothes off his body without him noticing," Abigail added with a charming smile.

"With the way that Mary was looking at him, he was so flustered he would've gladly given us his clothes without complaint!" Maria was as excited as the rest of us by how easy it all seemed.

Red and Frank made their way home about an hour after the twins arrived. They, like the rest of us, were just as thrilled by the ease of the operation. "How long do you think we have to wait for Ivan?" Red was quick to ask. "I don't like him being out there alone." No one did. It was nagging at the back of our minds, threatening to kill the happiness brought about by the mission's apparent success.

"I'm sure that Ivan will be just fine," Abigail reassured everyone. "He is certainly a rugged individual. His self reliance will see him through the day."

"What do we do if he still isn't back by tomorrow?" One of the twins asked quietly. Everyone looked to Abigail, our undisputed leader, for the answer.

"We go out and find him, simple as that. We tell Dime that he went missing and then we hunt him down," she was quick to respond. "Don't worry about it. Just wait, I bet he is home before midnight."

Midnight came and went without any word of Ivan. Everyone was getting nervous but none of us wanted to say what we were all thinking. We had promised ourselves that we wouldn't panic until sunrise the next day. That was still at least six hours away. Ivan should have plenty of time to return before then.

"Well," Maria said in a soft voice, "I have some hot chocolate powder saved from before our parents died that I was planning on making as a celebration, but I think we should just drink it now to cheer us up…" Her voice trailed off as she looked at the ground, appearing very small and childlike.

"Mary," Red said, accidentally using the wrong name, "that sounds like a fine idea. I will go help you make it. Should we heat it upstairs?" The girl nodded and began walking up the flight of steps to the water collection area with Red close behind. The rest of us made a very miserable and melancholy sight sitting around the empty fire pit, waiting for our friend we suspected was dead.

No one had even suggested eating that day. We were homeless, so a day without food was rarely something to notice, but eating with a friend lost in the field seemed like some kind of horrible blasphemy. Enjoying a meal without Ivan would have condemned him to death in all of our minds. Red and Maria were gone for a few moments and Abigail was just about to speak when we heard a knock on the door.

Chapter 10

The four of us in the kitchen froze in place, halting all movements except for the sharp turning of our heads toward the door. Was it the police? Was it Ivan? No one knew and none of us had any way of finding out that didn't involve going right up to the door to see. I stood up to go peer through the small peephole on the front of the door and check out our new visitor.

"No," Abigail grabbed me by the arm and pulled me back, "let me check it out. You need to get ready to run," she whispered, all seriousness. "Just in case," she winked.

I edged my way as silently as I could to the back door out of the kitchen that led to the woods, ready to use my powerful arm to force my escape. Mary grabbed the small pipe section the girls used as a weapon and I tossed my pistol to Frank. He took up position right behind Abigail, ready to shoot. The knocking came at the door again, louder than the first time. Abigail gulped down her fears and walked to the peephole in the door. After a second or two of looking outside her shoulders slumped and she unlocked the door, opening it.

Everyone was amazed and relieved to see Ivan standing there in the cold night air, waiting for us to open the door. He was wearing a big silly grin on his face and holding up the tiny sound recorder in his hand. "I gather from the amount of time that you guys spent in opening the door that you were a little afraid by my late arrival. Or perhaps you have just decided to kick me out of the group and want me gone. Shall I turn around and leave?" Ivan got us good, everyone in the kitchen was terrified, if only for a minute, but that terror gave way to joy and relief at the sight of Ivan in our doorway.

Abigail balled her hand into a fist and slugged Ivan right in the stomach, much to his surprise. "You had us scared to death! We thought you were dead out there!" she yelled at Ivan as he doubled over from the blow. She hadn't hit him hard though, it was more out of frustration than any real anger.

"Get in here, Ivan, let's see what gifts you might have brought us on that recorder," I yelled to him as I emerged from my position by the back door. Red and Maria came running down the stairs to greet Ivan with a handshake from the old veteran and a hug from the twin. We were so happy to see him alive that, despite his cruel joke, we couldn't stay angry at him for long. We were just glad to have him back. And with the recorder! It was a success to the fullest.

"So, tell us what happened, before Abigail beats you to death for scaring her," Mary asked, all of us eager to hear the information on the recorder. We sat down around the empty fire pit to hear the story, warmed by the hot chocolate in our hands. We didn't have any proper mugs to drink from so we had to use styrofoam cups that the women had taken from various drop-in shelters around town.

"I'm guessing that your new coat has something to do with your tardiness," Abigail said, the only one of us until then to notice the nice wool coat that Ivan was wearing over his rough street clothes.

Ivan laughed, "Indeed, this jacket used to belong to a certain Dr. Matthew J. Kowalski. I believe it was quite expensive when he bought it. Very nice fit, and the color is perfect, it compliments my style wonderfully. I'm glad you noticed my new, more sophisticated wardrobe." Ivan smiled as he brushed the coat down on his shoulders and showed off how nice it was.

"Ivan..." I was more than worried by that point, "you didn't.... you know, *kill* the doctor, did you?" Now I was nervous. If he killed the man, on purpose or accidentally, it could really step up the already intense investigation for our ragtag band. It would likely be the end of us, especially Ivan and I.

"Why, was I supposed to?" he grinned. "Of course I didn't kill the poor guy, I just stole his jacket! With the money I'm sure they pay him, he can afford another jacket." That was good, at least. Ivan didn't commit any murders while he was gone.

"Thank God," Red said, shaking his head.

"So, just to clarify for you guys, Dr. Kowalski works pretty late into the night. He didn't leave the building until just before midnight. That's why it took so long for me to get home, I wasn't going to leave without the recorder," Ivan began.

"When I saw the man coming out of the laboratory, I just followed him and staged a mugging. Well, I stole his coat and his wallet and his watch, so I guess I didn't really *stage* a mugging, I just mugged him. But anyways, I'm homeless, remember? Homeless people mug rich scientists all the time I bet. He won't suspect that the mugging is related to any of his work in the least. He has no idea that his jacket had the recorder on it the whole day so he probably just assumes that I stole his coat to keep me warm through winter. Brilliant, right?" It was, I had to admit. Ivan pulled off a brilliant retrieval of the sound recorder and scored a very handsome jacket in the process.

"You took his wallet?" Red asked, curious.

"And his watch, don't forget that, it's very nice, probably even real gold," Ivan replied, holding the watch out on his arm for all of us to admire. It was beautiful indeed and looked incredibly expensive.

"Was there anything interesting in his wallet? How much money did you get?" Mary asked excitedly.

"Well, he only had forty bucks on him, but we did get his credit cards, his driver's license with his address on it, and a plastic card that says Schwartz Laboratories, I'm betting that it will get us inside that building whenever we want."

"Unless he reports it stolen and they change the locks. I bet it's already been done." I said it under my breath, not wanting to kill the mood but unable to keep it simply to myself. "We probably shouldn't use the credit cards," I said out loud, not wanting anyone to get excited and spend a ton of money on our victim's credit line and bring more suspicion down upon us.

"Yeah, I know," Ivan said, still smiling. "We need to check out this sound recorder though, I'm dying to find out what it picked up. We only have one more shot at it if we didn't get enough information on this one to go to the police. Also, I'm starving. Can we get some dinner cooking in here?" he asked, rubbing his hands together as he spoke.

The twins stood up to get some food for us while Abigail retrieved the playback device. It took us a few minutes to figure out how to use a penny and a paperclip to create a makeshift screwdriver to remove the memory card from the device and insert it into the reader.

We had captured almost eighteen hours of sound with the device so it took us over a day to listen to it all. Most of it was just the sounds of typing, people walking, papers being shuffled around, books being taken off of the bookshelf and replaced, the secretary bringing in coffee and making small talk, the basic sorts of noises one would expect from an office environment anywhere.

About seven hours into the recording was our first bit of information. Dr. Kowalski was reading a report of some sort out loud to himself, editing it as he read. Though he was speaking softly and the jacket was most likely hanging on the coat rack in his room, far from his desk, what we were able to hear was very interesting.

"Mister... well, you don't tell anyone your name so it's hard to address things to you, now isn't it?" Dr. Kowalski was mumbling to himself as he corrected the title. "Major, I am pleased to report that the production of sarin gas..." The door to the office opened and a female voice came on next.

"Dr. Kowalski, we just received a message from the people working down below. They think they may have made a break through. You should get down there and check things out." Her voice was crystal clear, standing in the doorway.

"Radiation suit? The usual?" came the response from across the desk.

"Not this time. They said just wear these." There was a pause before Dr. Kowalski spoke again.

"What the hell? These are just lab goggles that someone has blacked out. I can't see anything in these. Are you sure?"

"Sir, they said it was imperative. I will instruct one of the blind men to lead you down. We should get going." The female voice sounded nervous, almost frightened.

"Alright, I understand. Let me..." The next part of the recording was too jumbled to understand.

It took a little over an hour for Dr. Kowalski to return. When he did, he returned in a flurry of excitement. The door swooshed open past the jacket on the coat rack and the sounds of Dr. Kowalski's footsteps were very hurried. He opened a few drawers on his desk in equal haste and it sounded like he was searching for something.

"Hello, Major? Okay, get me the Major." There was a pause of more than a minute, we could hear Dr. Kowalski impatiently tapping on his desk. "Tell him it's Dr. Kowalski, it can't wait, I have important news to tell him." Another pause, this one lasting twice as long. Everyone in the room listening to the recorder was on edge, waiting for the voice to return. "Then slide the damn phone under the stall door!" Dr. Kowalski was screaming at whomever he was speaking to. "I don't care if he is massaging Shakespeare's hairy ass, give him the damn phone before I have to come all the way down there and beat you until your bloody corpse agrees to hand him the phone!" Kowalski was yelling at the top of his lungs, making it rather easy to understand him on the recording.

"What kind of man reads Shakespeare when he's on the toilet?" Kowalski muttered, barely audible. "Yes, finally, Major..." he broke off. "Yes, I understand. This can't wait." Another long pause. It was clear from the footsteps on the recording that Dr. Kowalski was pacing. "Yes sir, I understand, just listen to me," another pause. Dr. Kowalski slammed his fist down on the desk and roared, "damn it, Major, we made a breakthrough! Just shut up and listen for once! We finished all the gas, we have a delivery system ready to go, and we finally know how it all works!" He was yelling into the phone, more out of excitement now than any real anger. "Yes! That is what I have been trying to tell you! Get down to the lab tomorrow, we just need a few more hours to perfect it." There was another long pause, maybe five minutes.

"You want..." The sound cut out again, briefly, "start human trials tomorrow? Are you nuts? Besides, I thought we already did a human trial. According to you, the little Vatican project went perfectly well." Everyone silently cheered. It was the confirmation that we had been looking for all along. They were behind the tragedy at Vatican City. Dr. Kowalski had confirmed the production of sarin gas. This was the evidence we needed.

"You realize that it will kill him, right?" Dr. Kowalski's voice came back, crystal clear. He must have been wearing the coat, getting ready to leave the office. "I understand. Have your goons bring me someone, I can't waste a valuable worker for a freak show." There came another long pause, filled only by footsteps. "Get the planes into position. We need all five to pull this off, you know that." Another short pause and the sound of a door opening. "Yes, tomorrow or the day after. I promise you, no one will suspect the ark for this." It sounded like Dr. Kowalski stopped moving for a moment. "Sarin gas has been used in plenty of terrorist attacks. It shouldn't be a problem to convince the media, they love this kind of sensational story." After another few moments of walking, Dr. Kowalski's voice came back, much quieter than before.

"Of course, I am certain. I wouldn't have called if I wasn't." It sounded like he was almost whispering as he said the words. "Look, you know why I'm helping you with this. Don't worry about me, I know what I'm doing. Everything is under control. No, they don't suspect anything." Another break in the speaking. "None of them. They are just as clueless as everyone else. See you tomorrow, Major. Thank you." It was another few hours before the recorder picked up anything else but none of it was very useful.

"So," I said, "I think this is enough to go to the police. What do you guys think?" I looked around the room at everyone's faces. Red was the only one shaking his head.

"I'm not sure we can afford to go to them just yet. What we have is good, but if these guys are as connected as I am betting they are, we might have our hands full at the police without something better to prove they killed all those people," Red said.

"From the sound of it, they plan on killing someone this very day for their little experiment or demonstration or whatever. We need to stop them. If we can prevent them from killing again and maybe even collect their intended victim as a witness, we should have more than enough to bring them down." Red was right, we couldn't risk going to the police with what we had. With the authorities almost certainly under the control of the Major, it was too risky to go to the police without hard physical evidence.

"I'm betting that the Major and Dr. Kowalski haven't told the police what's going on, at least not all of it. If we can get that guy they plan on killing, we might have enough information to take it to the police and prove our case." Red was sad as he said it, shaking his head. Our initial euphoria over Ivan's return dissipated fully when we realized that our evidence wasn't enough.

"Here, give me the recorder," Abigail reached out and took the small device from Ivan as she stood. "Follow me," she said, walking towards the basement door. The rest of us got up to follow without saying a word.

The dark basement was cold and moldy. Abigail led us down a small hallway beneath the house, one that was previously hidden from view by couple pieces of old plywood. I glanced back at Red to see him looking just as confused as I did, both of us wondering what the women were hiding behind their makeshift wall. Abigail took out the flashlight and shone it on the front of a small steel safe, mounted directly into the concrete foundation of the house. It was open with the door slightly ajar.

"What's in there?" I asked, my suspicion high.

"Nothing at the moment," Abigail replied, placing our one small piece of evidence inside the safe and pushing the heavy door closed. The safe had a heavy metal handle and a large black dial set into its face. Abigail gave the dial a spin, confirming that the safe was locked. She looked at the rest of us, standing there confused. "The twins and I know the combination. Now, we need to make our plan for finishing our mission. Let's discuss it upstairs."

"Hey," Frank said, pushing his way to the safe, "shouldn't we all get to know the combination? I mean, what if you three all get captured together?" It was a valid point, I had to admit.

"Yeah," Red agreed, "we should all know the combination, just in case." I nodded my agreement with Red, looking to Abigail expectantly.

"Alright, if you must know, it's just our birthdays. Mine, then the twins." The rest of us tried to memorize the code as best we could before concealing the safe once more.

Maria walked over to the storage area underneath the stairs and grabbed a large, flat piece of drywall. The twins placed the drywall against the wooden studs of the basement frame and used a small hammer to drive a few nails into the studs, securing it in place and completely disguising it.

Abigail ushered everyone up the stairs back to the ground floor as the twins replaced the plywood board over the opening to the hallway, further adding to the disguise.

We spent the next few hours of the day eating roasted bats and discussing our plans. None of us were really sure how we planned on getting more information without kidnapping Dr. Kowalski and beating the information out of him with a pipe, the plan suggested by Ivan and agreed to by the twins. Abigail, Red, Frank, and I didn't want to do anything that drastic. "Besides, that would just be a coerced confession, it would never hold up in court." That settled it. We couldn't just kidnap anyone and take the easy route out.

After a few painful hours of unproductive brainstorming, we simply decided to go back to Dime and ask him for help and advice. He knew the streets even better than Red and had some connections with the authorities that we might be able to exploit.

"Dime is a morning person," Red told us. "We should go meet with him first thing, at dawn, tomorrow morning." Everyone agreed. We were too exhausted from our emotional rollercoaster to think clearly that night anyways.

The group left the next morning, early enough to still be dark, Abigail and I volunteering to stay behind at the house. My plan was to finally talk to Abigail, alone, about what had happened between us upstairs as we had watched the man across the street being murdered by the police. I was young and inexperienced in where to even begin the conversation, but I wanted to get things cleared up between us before any sort of drama occurred that compromised anyone's safety. At least, that was the reason I told myself to rationalize everything. In all honesty, I liked her. I looked up to her as a leader and a trusted her with my life. Something inside couldn't allow me to just ignore the kiss she had given me; it was practically the only thing I thought about whenever I saw the woman.

The world was still heavy with the pre-dawn fog and darkness as the two of us sat around the smoldering embers in the fire pit. "So, how well *did* you know that guy across the street?" I asked, not sure how to bring up the subject of the kiss.

"He was just a friendly neighbor, really," she responded curtly. It was obvious from her tone and body language that she didn't want to talk about it. Not knowing what to say, I just let the question hang there in the awkward silence that followed.

"So, you were never married?" It was the best I could come up with. Alone, Abigail's good looks were intimidating. My eyes kept trying to stare at her even when my mind kept commanding them to just look into the remnants of the fire.

"I was engaged once, when I was eighteen. My parents didn't approve of the relationship on account of my age so we had to break it off." She didn't look at me while she spoke. She just stared around the room mindlessly, looking at everything but me.

"What was his name? What was he like?" I asked, trying to get her into a conversation that I could steer into a direction that I wanted.

"Look, Esau, I can see where you are going with all this." She looked me right in the eyes, unflinching. "I shouldn't have kissed you that day." I could feel my heart breaking with every syllable. "I was scared and I felt alone, and you reminded me of the person I once loved, my fiancé. I don't know why I did it, but we should just put it behind us. We have more important things to worry about than some high school romance drama."

I knew that I looked visibly hurt. I must have looked pathetic. Abigail stood up and started to go up the steps to the top floor.

She was halfway up the staircase when we heard the sirens. "Police," I said, rushing to the staircase on Abigail's heels, going to the upstairs window to look.

"That's a lot of police cars, Esau." Abigail was frightened, just like me. "They are coming for us this time." She was right. The cars were headed right for our house.

"No, they are only after me," I said, looking around frantically. "If you run now, you might make it. I have to get the evidence. This is it." I kissed Abigail on the forehead, "just in case," I said with a wink. We ran down the stairs as fast as we could. Abigail opened the front door and bolted, heading in the direction of Dime's bookstore and the rest of the group.

I tripped over my own feet and fell down the basement stairs, hitting my head hard on the bare concrete. I scrambled to my feet and tossed the plywood disguise aside and ran right for the drywall concealing the safe, my metal fist leading the way.

Why was the Major coming now? Who had tipped them off to my location? The sirens were wailing, filling my ears. A dull thud accompanied the high pitched notes of the siren, a battering ram, just like they had done across the street. I heard it hit once, a second time, the door wouldn't last long. They had me surrounded.

Chapter 11

The nurse stayed in the room for a while longer, shaking her head and just looking at me. She said that the Vatican had been 'blown up', what does that mean? Dr. Kowalski and the Major must have carried out their plan. I could see them detonating bombs filled with sarin gas over all of those dead bodies. Well, we never really thought we could prevent them from covering it up anyways.

Thankfully, the nurse left the room without realizing that I was awake.

I have to get out of this hospital. If I stay here, I'll be trapped forever and probably killed. Now that the authorities have gone public with their slaughter, they have the perfect scapegoat, handcuffed to a gurney, I realized, much to my dismay.

Only one of my arms was handcuffed to the gurney though. So they knew about the strength of my prosthetic. I looked around the room, searching for the missing limb. It was sitting on a small table to my left, by the only window in the room. It looked so pathetic sitting there, like something out of a comic book, like I was some sort of mutant criminal mastermind.

At least the arm was in the room, I wouldn't have to go searching for it when I made my escape. I could see the back of a police officer standing in front of the door to my room. It could be worse, I thought, he could be in here with me, watching my every move. So, they didn't expect me to wake up anytime soon, that was a good sign, I could take them by surprise.

I sat up in the bed, or at least I tried to. The pain in my back was unbearable. Had I been shot? Stabbed? It felt like my back was splitting in half as I tried to sit up. I looked around the room, searching for anything useful. There were x-rays on a board above my head.

I had to strain and twist my neck around far enough to get a glimpse of the pictures without blacking out from the pain in my back. From the angle, I wasn't able to see much, but I could tell that it was an x-ray of my stomach and chest area. The image on the left showed a bullet lodged in my gut. The x-ray on the right showed the same area after they took it out. "So I had been shot," I mumbled to myself, trying to remember everything that had happened. How long had I been handcuffed to the gurney?

I used what little wiggle room the handcuff provided to slide my gown up on my chest and get a look at the surgery site. I instantly regretted the decision, not having much of a stomach for wounds. There was a line of staples running from just below my right nipple half way down to my waistline. I had been shot in the back, yet had a massive scar on my chest. The bullet must have broken some ribs or something. Maybe it fragmented inside my body and they had to dig around the front of me to get all the little pieces. The thought made me shiver, and almost made me gag as well. I pulled the gown back down as best I could, not wanting to look at the gruesome scar any longer.

I felt a twinge in my neck and reflexively tried to bring my hand up to scratch it, only to jerk violently against the handcuff, sending a bolt of pain coursing through my back. Instinct made me try to send my right arm to find the scratch, only to feel the electrical signals stop abruptly in my shoulder. I had to get my right arm back. It attached easily enough, my natural arm ended just after the shoulder with a metal port that the arm clicked into. It was just a matter of three simple latches to lock it into place.

The nurse came back in the room. I closed my eyes and tried to assume as restive a pose as I could, fighting to ignore the itching in my neck. I wanted more than anything to just squirm around and rub my neck on the pillow. The nurse was doing something with the line hooked into my skin, probably replacing the bag of fluids hanging from the rack above me. I had to take a risk with the nurse.

"What are you giving me?" I asked in as small a voice as I could, not even opening my eyes. There was a pause, the nurse standing still, probably with her mouth open, staring at me in disbelief. "What is it?" I asked again, opening one eye to look her in the face and smile.

"Just... just something to keep you hydrated is all," she managed to stammer. One of her hands was dangling by her side, close to my handcuffed wrist. She turned to go out of the room, probably to alert the officers, and I grabbed her by the wrist.

"Please, don't leave me, not yet," I said, trying to sound as weak and scared as possible. I smiled at her and closed my eyes again, feeling her stay by my side.

"How do you feel?" the nurse asked. Her tone told me that she didn't expect my answer to be anything but pain.

"It hurts, but it isn't too bad. What happened to me?" I needed to get some information out of her and hopefully get her to reattach my arm.

"You were shot, um, well, I don't even know your name," she stammered. "The chart just says 'John Doe' but they usually only put that down for the deceased." Did they expect me to die in this hospital bed?

"You can call me Jacob," I said, figuring that since I was still alive, I deserved to have a nicer name. "Can you do me a favor, please?" I looked her right in the eye as I spoke, trying to gather every ounce of sympathy she might have for me.

"Well it is sure nice to meet you, Jacob. Do you want some water? Some food? Just tell me, sweetie." It worked. She had fallen for my young innocence, or so I hoped.

"My arm, my right arm," I pleaded, "it hurts when I don't have the prosthetic attached. I usually never take it off except to have it repaired." That part was true at least. "I need it back. Please?" I made my eyes water as I said it, not a difficult task considering the pain in my back.

"I don't know, Jacob," the nurse responded, "They told me not to let you have it. I should go get someone and have them make the decision." The police must have warned her about the arm, I was losing the nurse.

"Please, you have to understand," I begged, tears running down my cheeks, "I'm handcuffed to the bed, I just want my prosthetic, please, it will ease the pain." The nurse was shaking her head.

"If it hurts that much, let me up your dosage of morphine." She reached for the clipboard at the end of my bed.

"No, please, no more pain meds, I can't think straight when I take that much morphine, please." I let my eyes close and let a sob escape my lips, the heaving of my chest sending pain through my back.

The nurse let a long sigh out after a moment of contemplation. "Alright, but I'll have to take the arm back off when the police come in tonight to check on you."

Victory. I walked her through the steps to reattach my arm and then feigned relief when it was finally connected. I told her that it would take a few hours for the use of it to return to my body and she bought the lie. As soon as the metal was synched into the computer system buried under the skin of my shoulder I could feel the power of the arm, ready to use at my command. The feeling in my brain was jolting at first, like always, but then comfortably familiar. When I had first gotten my prosthetic it had taken me months to be able to reconnect it without screaming, the mental shock of the computer system turning on was nearly unbearable. I learned to control it over the years, to let the system come online as quickly as possible but directing my mental energy away from that part of my body.

I let my arm lay limp against my side, fully convincing the nurse that it wasn't a threat. When the nurse was leaning over my body reattaching my arm, I had managed to read her name tag. "Thank you, Sister Francesca," I said, "will you pray over me?" I was hoping to play to her softer sympathies. It worked beautifully.

"God bless you," I said as Sister Francesca left the room. "Don't tell anyone you did this for me, I don't want you to get in trouble for my sake." The kind nurse smiled and just shook her head as she exited the room, oblivious to how well she had played into my cunning.

A different nurse came in later with a tray of food, indicating that Sister Francesca had told at least one person that I had woken up. The police hadn't arrived though, that was good. I didn't realize how incredibly hungry I was until I saw the tray of hospital food sitting in front of me. Sister Francesca hadn't handcuffed my right arm to the bed so I was able to eat with relative ease. The warm buttered noodles tasted like cardboard and the applesauce could easily have been made from rotten apples but I devoured it all in a frenzy. At least the water they gave me was cold and refreshing.

After the empty food tray was taken away I decided to make a move. Sister Francesca had told me that the police were coming in to check on me every night. They would surely suspect that something was amiss if they saw my arm reattached and I had no intentions of letting the nurses remove it ever again.

I grabbed the handcuff firmly with my metal hand, judging the strength of my shackles. I knew I could break these cuffs. I tried to pull them apart by slipping two fingers inside the loop and pushing them apart but even my strength couldn't do anything from that angle. I gripped the bottom of the handcuffs, right below my wrist and began to squeeze them shut, knowing that if I could crush the locking mechanism inside the cuff by forcing it against my wrist I could probably slip out.

My fist began to clench down on the metal, squeezing it painfully into my wrist. The skin of my left arm started to break as the cuff tightened around my wrist and blood began to trickle down my arm and onto the white sheets. I grimaced against the pain, knowing that it would be much worse without the morphine in my system. I heard the lock inside the cuff starting to crack and break and I squeezed all the harder, feeling the power in my arm.

The lock gave way as I released the handcuff and watched the crushed metal fall the floor. I was free. My wrist was bleeding freely from both sides, but I was free. A flick of my hand had the needle from the bag suspended above my head dangling and dripping liquid onto the floor. I got up as quickly as my wounded back would let me and rummaged through the drawers in the room until I found a bandage. After I wrapped my wrist in clean white cloth I found my clothes sitting on the windowsill. I growled away the pain as I pulled the pants onto my legs. The shirt was a just as painful. I couldn't lift my real arm above my head, the pain was so great.

I used my metal hand to touch the back of my neck, noticing a small bump to the side of my spine. The cold feeling from the night I was captured came rushing back. The Major had placed what I thought was the barrel of his gun against my neck and it had frozen the sweat to my skin it was so cold.

My fingers could feel something under the skin, some small object. He must have injected me with something and used the cold to numb the area and try to trick me. Whatever it was, if the Major had placed it there, it had to go. I found a small pair of delicate yet sharp scissors in the drawer I had found the bandages and I sat down in the windowsill, bracing myself and steeling my nerves for an attempt at amateur surgery.

The blade of the scissors pierced the skin much easier than I expected. Blood immediately began to flow down my neck, causing me to promptly regret putting my shirt on before the surgery attempt.

There was a large mirror in the room but my neck hurt too much to turn my head and look as I carved my skin away. I had to do it all by the feel of a metallic hand. My initial cut created two small holes about an inch apart, just to the right of my vertebrae. With the scissor tips still an eighth of an inch deep into the flesh of my neck I closed the grip, cutting a straight line between the holes. A rush of warm blood spilled to the floor and my vision started to go dark, waves of pain washing over my mind.

I doubled over in agony, hardly believing that such a small cut could possibly hurt as much as it did. Trying to create some sort of mental bulwark to ward off the physical torment, I used my natural arm to brace myself against the window frame and catch my breath. I was losing a lot of blood, I knew. This surgery needed to end quickly.

I moved the scissors back to my neck, fear and the pulsing pain in my body slowing my hand to a crawl. I felt the slot I had created with the tip of the scissors. It was deep, but it didn't touch anything foreign as far as I could tell. Thinking that my pain couldn't possibly get any worse than it already was, I reached my left hand up to my neck, getting ready to investigate the inner workings of my spine for whatever the Major may have placed there. With the tip of the scissors firmly embedded inside the thick meat of the back of my neck I opened my hand, spreading the skin wide, creating a window.

I was wrong. The pain was unbelievable, unlike anything I had ever experienced. It burned and throbbed, every pulse sending a wave of my fresh blood splattering onto the floor. The warm, sticky liquid making its way down my back and into the top of my pants nearly made me vomit. I started to heave and the spasm of my chest made me drop the scissors into the thick pool of blood at my feet. I clamped my hand over the incision, trying to stem the flow of blood while I reached down and retrieved the now thoroughly soaked and slippery improvised scalpel. I grit my teeth as hard as I could and opened the cut on my neck again, plunging my natural fingers into the cut, feeling for any sort of hard object.

It's an eerily unique feeling, having your own fingers poking around inside your body, bloody up to the knuckles. The sucking and squishing sounds my fingers made every time they moved under my skin was enough to churn my stomach and make me heave again, breaking my concentration.

I pushed my fingers in deeper, farther to the right, and sent another spurt of warm blood cascading down my neck. I felt something. My fingers were too far to the right of my neck for it to be the bones of my spine. Not having any medical experience, I could only hope that what I felt wasn't my spinal column.

Reaching farther into the cut, I pinched the edge of whatever it was between my fingertips. The slick blood made it hard to get a solid grip but I was able to move the object just slightly. Another wave of pain hit me. I doubled over, sheer concentration keeping me from ripping my hand away from my neck and passing out. The hospital bed was tempting, inviting me to just lie down and sleep, letting the blood from my neck slowly seep out until there was none left. I couldn't do it though, I told myself. I had friends still out there, still fighting. I could feel the object coming loose under my skin so I made one final pull, wrenching it free of its bloody shell.

The warm wave of my lifeblood that followed the tiny object was dizzying. I fell to the ground, grabbing the back of my neck and clamping it as hard as I could, trying to stem the flow before I passed out and died. Trying not to scream was the hardest part. I couldn't just alert the guard outside to what I was doing.

Lying there, in a pool of my own blood, I curled up, trying to defend myself against the constant onslaught of unbearable pain. I threw the scissors across the room, trailing blood along the white sheets of my bed. I knew I couldn't lie there on the floor much longer. My body was losing blood every second and a nurse would likely be in my room to check on me at any moment.

I slowly sat up, leaning my back against the wall beneath the window, my vision blurry, clouded by alarmingly large black spots. My heart was racing, pounding violently in my chest, as though I had just sprinted a mile. I was exhausted, mentally and physically. I stood up and made my way stumbling back to the drawer and took out a large roll of sterile white gauze. I wrapped the roll as tightly as possible around my neck several times, feeling the pressure begin to stymie the flow of blood.

I pocketed the rest of the gauze and sat down to catch my breath and slow my heart rate before making my escape. The bag of clear liquid connected to the intravenous line was on a mobile metal pole with wheels. I put the needle in my hand against the pole, not wanting to try to reinsert it for the sake of disguise, and I made my way to the door, peering out the small square window. There was an officer sitting in a chair, appearing to be asleep. It was late at night and from what the nurse said, no one expected me to wake up this soon, I couldn't blame the officer for his laxity on the job. In fact, I silently thanked him for it.

I pushed the door open as silently as I could and hobbled out, pushing the bag in front of me. Sadly, the officer wasn't carrying a gun. He did have a small can of pepper spray that I managed to steal without him noticing. I started shuffling slowly down the hallway, trying to be as inconspicuous as possible. I was halfway to the elevator when Sister Francesca turned the corner, coming right towards me. My head was already down, hiding my face, and I simply did a full turn and started to shuffle off faster in the other direction. The nurse was reading some document, probably a medical chart, and never even looked down the hallway to see me.

I kicked up my pace as fast as my wounded neck and back would allow without causing me to scream in pain, my vision still less than normal. I walked back past the door to my room, just ten paces ahead of the nurse. I couldn't help but smile when I turned the corner of the hallway and heard poor Sister Francesca scream at the top of her lungs. I had done nothing to hide the gratuitous volume of blood I had spilled; the room looked like a murder scene. I could make out the heavy footsteps of the police officer rushing into the room.

Luck was with me as I turned that corner. Not only was an elevator right in front of me, it was an open elevator, a trio of young children exiting and talking happily amongst themselves. I passed them and entered the elevator, the doors closing just in time for me to smile at the police officer rushing around the corner. Standing up, the officer was much taller than he appeared and, from the looks of it, he was in excellent physical shape. The look in his eyes told me that the chase was on and that it was going to be a tough one.

Reading the number off the sign in the elevator lobby, I learned I was on the fifth floor. My hand instinctively went for the button for the ground floor but I didn't push it. The cop would expect that. Instead, I reached up and pushed the button for the seventh floor, thinking to use a little deception to my advantage.

I got out on the seventh floor, ditched my bag on a pole in the nearest open room and walked briskly up to a nurse's station. I turned the corner around the station and grabbed a white doctor's coat off a hanger as I did, slipping it quickly over my shoulders. Worried that I would be seen and suspected, I walked quickly to the next group of elevators and waited for one to arrive. Standing there, waiting for the elevator, I realized that my coat had a name tag on it identifying me as Doctor Honsey. That was good, I had an identity. I was lucky the coat had a European name on it and I didn't accidentally grab a coat from anyone named Lopez or Yatsumoto.

The elevator doors opened and an incredibly old man started wheeling himself out of the elevator in a wheel chair. Thinking on my feet, I looked at him and smiled. "Mr. Jones, just where do you think you're going?" I exclaimed, using a cheesy but friendly voice. I grabbed the handles of the wheel chair and spun the man around, pushing him right back into the elevator.

I pressed the button for the second level of the parking garage, assuming the majority of the police would be on the main floor. Using the collar of the coat to hide the bloody bandages on the back of my neck, I practiced my best doctor pose. The reflection in the elevator doors wasn't very much to go by but I told myself that I looked convincing. The elevator doors opened on the ground floor, much to my horror.

There were cops everywhere, at least a dozen of them. As soon as the doors opened, a few of them turned my way but none of them took much notice. A nurse stepped into the elevator and pressed the button for the first level of the parking garage.

"Hello," I said, trying to seem casual.

"Hi," she responded, staring ahead at the doors, obviously not interested in making any small talk. The doors opened again at the parking garage and she stepped out without another word spoken between us.

The elevator opened once more, on the second floor of the subterranean garage and I stepped out, pushing the button to send the elevator and the old man back to floor seven, where he belonged. "Where are you going, doctor?" The old man called after me.

"I have some unfinished business to take care of," I called back, "and so do you."

Chapter 12

The Major woke up in a haze, his head pounding with a brutal hangover. He had slept on the couch again, for the third day in a row. Empty bottles of peppermint schnapps were strewn all about the floor of the small apartment. Cartoons were blaring on the television in Spanish, painfully stinging the Major's sensitive ears. Luckily for him, the lights were turned off and the shades were shut.

He looked around the small apartment, frantically trying to find the remote to turn off the television. After a few futile moments of searching he stood up, wearily stretching his sore back. The Major nearly tripped over an empty bottle of schnapps as he made his way across the room to the metal trash can in the corner.

The remote always made its way to the trash can when he was drinking.

Retrieving the remote and finally turning off the television, the Major began to think back on what he remembered from the last few days. Ever since Captain McCreary had told him where the kid was being held, the Major had relaxed. He drank himself to sleep every night, spent his entire days lounging around his apartment, usually naked, spending a few hours each night to check in with Dr. Kowalski. Everything had gone right in the Major's mind.

"We've unlocked the secrets to the ark, staged a terrorist attack, and captured the primary suspect without a single casualty. I should be president by now, not letting my talents go to waste in this trash heap we call a city," the Major mumbled to himself as he found his clothes piled up in a heap on the floor. Oddly enough, his pearl-handled revolver was still in its holster, strapped to his unclothed side.

The doorbell rang. "Yeah, yeah, give me a minute," the Major called out, buttoning his shirt and starting to tuck it into his khakis. He opened the door a moment later, squinting away the pain of the bright afternoon sun, and saw a very terrified teenage pizza delivery boy standing before him.

"Sorry to bother you sir, but you placed this order last night, said to deliver it at one o'clock this afternoon," the scared boy opened the box to present the pizza. "Banana peppers, onions, and bacon, sir, just like you ordered." It was the same pizza boy that always came to his door after the Major drank.

The Major grabbed the pizza from the boy, causing him to shrink back in terror at the disheveled yet imposing figure. "Well, at least I have the good sense to order some food when I'm drunk. Pizza has always been the best hangover cure," the Major said under his breath as he tossed a twenty dollar bill to the delivery boy and slammed the door.

He ate half of the pizza, took a few doses of headache medicine, and started out the door, not bothering with a shower, shave, or fresh clothes. It didn't take long to hail a taxi once he was down on the street. "Saint Hubert of Liege Hospital," he told the cab driver, relaxing his still pounding head on the soft leather seats.

The Major stepped out of the cab twenty minutes later in front of the monolithic hospital. "So, this is where you lie, defeated and alone," he said, smiling as he walked in. The hospital, the largest in the city, was built like the Washington Monument. There was a helipad built to one side of the parking lot but other than that, the only building was the hospital itself, towering above the city. It reached thirty stories into the sky, looking more like an insurance company headquarters than a medical facility.

"I'm with the police department," he told the front desk secretary, flashing his badge. "I'm looking for a young male, came in here a few days ago with a gunshot wound, still under confinement." The middle-aged woman typed a few things into her computer.

"We have him on the fifth floor, sir, room 539. The elevator to your left will take you there." The woman smiled as the Major walked away towards the elevator. He arrived on the fifth floor to see a police cordon and a dozen officers standing around, talking to the crime scene investigators.

"Oh no. No, no, no. You cannot be serious," the Major roared as he exited the elevator, "one little kid! That's all you had to guard, one little teenage brat! He was handcuffed to the bed! How could you let him escape?" Everyone was stunned into silence by the fiery and unexpected arrival of the Major. The angry man took a few quick steps past the police line and walked into the hospital room. Yelling made the Major squint, fighting off the pain in his head.

"How many of the hospital staff did he murder?" The Major asked. He acted like the amount of blood in the room didn't surprise him one bit. "Looks like two nurses, I'm guessing. With this much blood though, he must have had a weapon." He looked to the crime scene investigator kneeling by the window sill.

"Here," the man responded, holding up an evidence bag containing a bloody pair of scissors, "we found these. Pretty gruesome work for a seventeen year old kid. The thing is, none of the hospital staff has been reported missing or injured. All of this blood is his, as far as we can tell." The investigator sounded just as confused as the Major felt. There was blood everywhere, pooled by the window, splattered against the walls, soaking the sheets of the bed.

"You're telling me that one person, a kid, lost this much blood, and still managed to escape? I don't buy it. Is anything missing from the room?" The Major was calm, thoroughly perplexed by the situation and trying his best to think it through, despite his hangover.

"Well, he took his clothes and his arm of course, only thing missing from the room was a roll of gauze and the fluid drip stand that held his lines. Want to see something more bizarre? Check out the handcuffs on the bed." The investigator tapped the bloody railing with his gloved hand, showing the major the crushed pieces of metal tangled up in the bloody hospital sheets.

"It looks like someone put the bottom of the cuffs in a vice and just crushed it until it broke," the Major said, moving the sheets to get a better view of the broken cuffs. The two men just shook their heads, not know what else to say. "Have you gotten anything from the security cameras?" the Major asked, hoping for some bit of good news.

"Yeah, the footage from the hallway cameras is still being checked out but we see him escaping. We don't know what happened in the room though. One minute the room is quiet, nothing happening, then all of a sudden the kid emerges from the room, covered in blood, with a bandage around his neck." The officer sounded as though he himself had a hard time believing what he was saying.

"Anything that points to some sort of struggle? Did anyone else enter the room?"

"No," the investigator responded, "the blood here is pooled, not splattered. I would say that the victim, or however we want to label him, was holding still when it happened, and if it was this pair of scissors that did the job, it was done slowly and deliberately. Honestly, this blood pattern is very indicative of a suicide. Only suicide cases usually leave a body at the scene..." So it had been done on purpose, deliberately.

Then it clicked in the Major's head. The transmitter! The kid must have felt the transmitter embedded under his skin and used the scissors to cut it out. "Alright, I've seen enough of this blood bath. If you figure out anything new, be sure to tell me immediately." The Major handed the young crime scene investigator a card with his number on it and walked out of the room, suspecting that he knew exactly where the kid had gone to hide.

The Major walked the few blocks to the police station, bundled up against the cold. He wondered if the police would find the small transmitter in the room or if the kid had thought to take it with him. No, he concluded, the kid would have likely destroyed it, not knowing what it was. He stopped at a convenience store before entering the station, using their bathroom to wash the blood from the hospital sheets off of his fingertips. He bought a small pack of overpriced antacids, chewed a few and walked into the station, wondering what he would say.

"You failed," the Major said as he opened the door, calmly striding through. All the eyes in the room were upon him, waiting for him to explode in one of his usually bursts of rage. "We can salvage this though," the Major continued, keeping his calm.

"Send two patrol cars back to the house, round up everyone who is dumb enough to still be there. Bring them down for questioning. This may come as a surprise to some of you, but the Red Baron, one of your most loyal informants, has a son working out on the streets, helping this kid out. We need to bring him down. I need a cruiser to take me to the used book store down on Vine Street, it's past time that we made use of this Jericho, instead of letting him just be some idol of the homeless scum walking the streets." An officer on an unrelated case had reported yesterday that a group of homeless were gathering by the used bookstore, the well known haunt of the street urchin Jericho.

The police station exploded into action, officers running to their cars, scrambling to put on bulletproof vests. The police cruiser barreled down the streets, lights flashing and sirens blaring, taking the Major to the book store. Officers rushed out of the cars, surrounding the old building, weapons drawn. The Major walked up to the door and peered inside, not seeing any movement.

He motioned for one of the officers to open the door and lead the charge, fully expecting the ragtag group of homeless people to open fire. The police poured into the building, moving from bookshelf to bookshelf, shouts ringing out between them, coordinating their scan of the room. No one was in the building. The back room was equally deserted.

The Major grabbed the radio from the shoulder of the nearest officer, forcefully yanking the officer to his side in the process. "Has anyone found him? Tell me you have this kid, tell me!" The officer attached to the radio flinched at the volume of the Major's voice so close to his ear, more than a little spit hitting his face. There was static, no officer responding on the other side of the radio transmission.

The Major began to storm away, out of the bookstore when the voice finally came over the radio. "Nothing sir, we found nothing. The house is empty. No sign of the kid or his friends. We're heading home, sir." The Major heard the words as he walked out of the building, his head hanging low.

"I want two plain clothes officers here until we catch them. That kid shows his face here, take him down. Step up the patrols around that house, rustle up some other homeless people, ask questions, we need to find this kid!" The Major felt it, time was running out. He needed to catch this kid, again, and soon.

Yesterday, he had been ready to go to the media with their story, the story of how this young rebel, influenced by a terrorist cell operating right in this city, was the keystone to a sarin gas attack that destroyed Vatican City. The media would have devoured the story without a doubt. They loved the sensational emotion that only a young, American terrorist can bring.

It was always easy to convince the news stations of any lie as long as it was an American that played the part of the villain. The Major spit on the sidewalk, thinking about the media's relentless anti-Americanism made his stomach churn and furled his brow.

"Take me to Schwartz Laboratories," the Major commanded as he sat down in the passenger seat of a cruiser. He stared out the window, watching the grimy streets and the abandoned buildings roll by. The kid could be anywhere, he knew. If his little group of friends was working in concert with Jericho, it could prove impossible to find him again. The police had gotten lucky those few days ago, catching the kid unaware. One of the local patrols had seen some activity in the house and had decided to call it in. They just happened to be right.

The Major got out of the police car, slamming the door shut behind him. He stalked up the pathway to the entrance of the lab and waited impatiently for the door to be unlocked.

The secretary wasn't at her desk. All the lights were on, the computers were on, but the lab was silent. As soon at the Major walked into the building he drew his revolver, sensing the tension in the air. Something was wrong. Where had the secretary gone?

The Major did a quick scan of the room, looking for signs of a struggle or blood. Nothing was out of place, no desk overturned, no papers strewn about the floor. Everything looked eerily calm. There should always be a secretary, the Major thought. He gently patted the pocket of his jacket, reassuring himself with the feel of bullets. If the kid was currently in the laboratory, the Major intended to kill him, no questions asked.

He walked slowly down the hallway to Dr. Kowalski's door, knocking gently before testing the handle. No response came from the other side of the heavy door, but it was unlocked. The Major slowly edged the door open, his antique pistol leading the way. Swinging the door open fully and bursting into the room, the Major saw books and papers strewn all over the floor. The desk was pushed over, the chair was on its side, the office looked like a warzone. "No blood," the Major whispered to himself, "that's one good sign at least."

He stayed in the ruined office for a few short moments, looking for bullet casings, holes in the walls or furniture, anything that would indicate violence. Dr. Kowalski's letter opener, shaped like an Indonesian kris, was the only weapon to be found in the office. It was clean, no signs of blood anywhere near it, still sitting in its ornate holder. The Major continued to creep down the hallway towards the stairs leading to the bowels of the building. Voices could be heard from the cathedral section of the laboratory. The Major snuck up to the door silently, listening, trying to pick out the voices, hoping that he wasn't too badly outnumbered.

There was a heated argument taking place in the room. Dr. Kowalski's voice rose above the rest, "we may have to kill," he said as the others went quiet. Kill whom? Why? Questions raced through the Major's mind. He stood tall and pushed the door open, walking right into the center of the room, pistol in his hand at his side. Dr. Kowalski, a handful of scientists, and three of the monks were standing in the room, all eyes upon their newest guest. "Major…" Dr. Kowalski managed to stammer, obviously at a loss for words.

"Who might we need to kill?" The Major asked, remembering the absence of the secretary, "not that young girl who sits behind the front desk, I hope." The Major returned his pistol to its holster, seeing that none of the men in the room were armed.

"No, no, of course not, sir." Dr. Kowalski was clearly frightened, on edge. "We were all just discussing our options. We heard that the witness escaped. I..." He paused, nodding to the rest of the men assembled, "and the rest of the staff believes that it is time to do the same. That secretary, she left a few days ago, she kept talking about some sort of break in, but our guards never reported anything. See Major, this whole thing is falling apart on top of us. I don't want to be stuck trying to climb out of the rubble of your legacy." There it was. The team was coming apart, the project was over. They had lost faith.

"So, it comes down to this. We have one little hiccup and you jump ship. Where will you go? Even if this does come down on our heads, where will you hide? I could rat every single one of you out to cover my own tail, and don't think I won't. You have nowhere to run and no way to possibly cover for yourselves. I could have every single person in this room killed." He patted his weapon for effect. The confident demeanor of the Major pushed everyone back a step. He spoke with such a calm tone that no one dared to doubt his words.

"I'm going to Argentina," Dr. Kowalski said, trying to get control of his shaking voice. "My grandfather fled to Argentina back when I was just a little kid. I still have some family there. The bottom line is, Major, we don't want to go down in flames with you and your plan. We tried, it failed, we're out. That's the end of it. You had your chance to make it all work, you had the kid. He slipped through your fingers and now we have to run to make sure we don't become the next scapegoat." The scientists were nodding their agreement. Oddly enough, the monks looked as though they were not even listening and cared little about what was happening. The Major couldn't decide if that was a good or bad thing.

"And you three, I suppose that you intend to leave for South America as well?" The Major looked right into the white eyes of the blind monks but had to look away. Their gaze, blind as it was, was nearly unbearable. The eyes of the blind monks penetrated and scrutinized anything they looked at with a mystical energy that sent fear into even the Major's cold heart.

"We all travel with the ark. Where it goes, so too shall we follow, always with the ark. That is our place." The cryptic monk's answer was predictable and infuriating.

"Take me to it," the Major said, pointing at the door. "I want to see how it works. I want to see it with my own eyes." The monks moved to the door without a word. The youngest one of the old group opened the door with a loud sigh. The heavy stone door, with the word *Petra* carved into its center, opened slowly and silently.

The Major had been tracking the artifact hidden behind that door for decades, using every resource he could to find it. It hadn't taken the team long to realize what mysteries the door itself held. The Major's team of scientist and archaeologists had been searching the region of Mount Hor, Jordan, for indication of the tomb and shrine of Miriam, the sister of Moses. They were following an old legend that said the Ark of the Covenant had been sunk into the natural spring that marked the place of Miriam's death.

Suspecting that the spring had since dried up, the team used long metal rods to take cores out of the mountain and test for water deposits. After one such core was taken, on the mountain near Al Dier, water started to pour forth from the ground and well up all around the feet of the scientists. The water kept coming, forming a steady stream that flowed all the way to the base of the Al Dier monastery. After two days of excavating, the team had discovered that the section of mountain top they were standing upon was actually the ceiling of a large underground cave. The cavern was entirely flooded but it didn't take much to drain the water and divert the spring away from the cave. The Major and one other scientist, Dr. Kowalski, had dropped into the cave to explore it personally, instructing the rest of the team to remain on the top of the mountain, waiting.

The first chamber of the cave was perfectly square with the heavy stone door set into one wall, the word *Petra* glistening in the center of the door. The Latin inscription, *"Lux in Tenebris"*, had obviously been added above the door some time after the chamber had been constructed. Dr. Kowalski had been the one who pushed the door open. It didn't make a sound, but the chamber had filled with light when the door swung open. It wasn't light from the room behind the door, it was light coming from above, from the opening in the ceiling of the chamber. It was as though the clouds had moved and the most intense sunlight in the entire world had poured into the chamber, illuminating everything.

The Major and Dr. Kowalski had found the Ark of the Covenant behind that door. It was being watched over by seven blind monks, old enough to have been from the original tribes of Moses. Water glistened off the walls of the cavern, making the light from the four braziers in the corners of the room shimmer and dance. The cavern wasn't very large, but something about the beauty of the place gave the impression that it was larger than any room on earth. Anyone standing in the chamber for long would feel insignificant and pathetic in comparison to their surroundings.

Living quarters were carved directly into the Eastern wall for the seven monks to sleep. There was a podium, facing the entrance to the chamber, with a book set upon it, its pages oddly blank. A natural spring fed the small underground pond in the very center of the chamber. It was in the middle of that pond that the Ark of the Covenant floated, seeming to be held up by magic.

"The tomb of Miriam," Dr. Kowalski gasped, stunned by the beauty of the room. "It's so much more magnificent than I had ever dreamed." The pair spent hours in the room, just standing in front of the podium and the monks, taking it all in.

When the Major left the cavern, followed closely by Dr. Kowalski, something strange had happened. He walked right out of the cavern and up the makeshift stairs, to the top of Mount Hor. He looked behind him, reaching a hand down to his friend to help him out, only to see that Dr. Kowalski was nowhere to be found. He waited by the entrance to the chamber, setting up a tent and folding chair, waiting for him. It was seven days to the minute before Dr. Kowalski emerged, completely oblivious to the amount of time it had taken him to leave the complex.

It took a few experiments with the local workers over the course of the next month to finally determine that touching the door to the chamber had its cost: seven days of time. Upon attempting to climb out to the mountain top, the workers who had touched the door simply disappeared and then came back seven days later, clueless.

Removing the door and retrieving the ark took nearly two months and almost bankrupted the operation. If it wasn't for the wildly successful business ventures of the Kowalski family, it would have been prohibitively expensive to move everything. The seven monks, without saying a word, followed the ark relentlessly. Dr. Kowalski and the Major were busy constructing a place for the ark to remain while they tested it when the monks arrived at the door to the laboratory, somehow making it all the way from Jordan to the United States in a couple of days. Seeing no reason to kill the monks or otherwise remove them, the two had simply reconstructed the cavern beneath the premises of Schwartz Laboratories, allowing the monks to continue their vigil.

It was several weeks later that the monks began to speak, to tell the secrets of the ark. They spoke an archaic version of English, leading everyone to believe that they were some sort of Teutonic knights from an age long ago. The Major had argued for just propping the door to the chamber open so that no one had to sacrifice their time just to run a simple test or speak with the monks but they had insisted that the door be shut when not in use, saying that to gaze upon the ark should always cost the most valuable resource known to man: life. It was also apparent that the monks themselves paid with their vision to be with the artifact, their lives seemingly endless anyways.

Heeding the advice of the monks, Dr. Kowalski and the Major had been in a different city the first time the ark had been opened. The two had ordered the monks to open the ark for a total of one second before replacing the lid. The entire team of scientists was in the room to watch, except for Dr. Kowalski of course. When the Major returned, everyone in the room was dead, save the monks. Immediately, the value of the ark as a weapon was realized. The two hired a new team of scientists and began trying to solve the mystery of the ark's power. Their plan was simple, if they could effectively use the ancient artifact as a weapon against entire cities, like a silent nuclear bomb, they could essentially rule the entire world through fear.

Their first two or three public attacks had to be staged like terrorist attacks to establish their power and willingness to use it before openly coming out to hold the world hostage. If they were discovered too soon, the governments of the entire world would align to stop them. The plan required a well established fear to be in place before anything was announced about the artifact. If this witness, however he survived the attack, was able to bring substantial evidence against the Major and Dr. Kowalski proving that they were behind the attacks, it would be impossible to use the ark as a weapon again. Everything hinged on getting the one survivor, dead or alive.

Now, it appeared, the entire team was abandoning the project. The monks led the Major and the other scientist down the carved stone steps to the watery chamber that housed the ark. The way in which the fire from the braziers in the corners of the room reflected off the beautiful object floating in the pool made everyone speak in whispers when they entered the cavern. It was almost as though any sort of loud noise would awake the ark and anger it, causing it to destroy everyone in the room.

"Alright, show me how this bloody thing works," the Major instructed, gazing up to the ceiling, noticing a mechanical arm newly set into the stone. There was another piece of new construction in the dank cavern, a small glass room with two rows of seats was set into the wall opposite the one used for the monks sleeping area.

"One demonstration, that's all you get, Major." Dr. Kowalski's tone wasn't overtly angry, just disappointed. "Let's get behind the glass," he said, ushering everyone into the small room. Two of the scientist began placing rodents in small cages at intervals from the pool of water to the glass room.

"How thick is this glass? It's hard to even see through it. I thought the ark didn't make any sort of explosion, right? Just a silent death? Why do we need the twelve inch thick bomb shelter glass?" The Major tapped on the glass wall, smiling at first, but then noticing tiny waves emanating out from the epicenter of his knock, like the entire wall was made of some sort of strange liquid material. "What... what is this wall made of? And the door too?" the Major asked, tapping on the door to notice the same strange effect.

"Just take a seat, Major," Dr. Kowalski said, his arm outstretched, pointing into the room. The Major took the first seat he came to, sitting down with his mouth hanging open, looking at the walls, the ceiling, it was an entire box made of the strange glass.

"I feel like I'm visiting an aquarium and a shark is about to swim over my head," the Major whispered, in awe of the room and not understanding it in the least.

"Well, that's almost correct. These walls are basically made of thin aquariums. Four inch thick ballistic glass holding a column of water, one foot deep, all around us." The Major gestured to all the walls, knocking on the front wall and sending ripples through it. "The monks have been very reluctant to share any information with us, but what we have been able to glean is that water prevents the death from spreading, hence the pool of water under the ark." The two scientists placed the last of the caged rodents inside the glass chamber and shut the door, locking it into place. As soon as the door was fully latched, a barrier between the door and wall dissolved, allowing the water from the door and the walls to mix, creating a perfect water barrier all the way around the observing group.

Dr. Kowalski moved to a small control panel on a pedestal behind the seats. Fire in the main chamber was the only source of light for the underground complex, giving the watery room an incredibly eerie aura of ominous silence. "Now, I'll try to explain what little I know about the ark. It isn't some sort of religious magic or the hand of God himself that comes down from the heavens to kill everything near the ark when it's opened. If it was, I doubt the water would help." One of the scientists chuckled, breaking at least some of the tension.

"During one of our experiments," Dr. Kowalski explained in hushed tones, "we were able to capture some of what comes out of the ark. It took a while to create a small containment device surrounded by water so that we could keep hold of the slippery gas."

"Wait, its gas? Wouldn't any sort of gas have deteriorated or dissipated or just be inert by now? Isn't this thing thousands of years old?" The scientists just shook their heads.

"One would think, but as of now, we have no idea what is even in the ark. We tried to throw a camera into it with a robotic arm but the camera turned to ash. Even when we did it with a water casing, we got the same result. Just doesn't work. Anyways, the gas is a pretty straightforward nerve agent, similar to VX, but a million times more toxic," Dr. Kowalski explained, trying to put his knowledge into terms that the Major could understand. That was always the trickiest part for an accomplished chemist, trying to explain things to people with no working scientific intellect.

"Think of it kind of like a virus, Major," the doctor continued. "When the gas is released, it absorbs the atoms around it, pulling them in and rearranging their subatomic structures to basically create copies. When the lid is replaced, the gas seems to lose its effect and simply dissipates." The Major was shaking his head in disbelief, not really understanding the science behind the explanation.

"That is how the gas moves and multiplies so rapidly," he explained, "moving through the air, infecting everything. We suspect that it is capable of moving through water and seems to move through other liquids with ease, but that is where it gets a little tricky. It is like the gas itself is a living organism and makes the conscious choice to not have any effects on water, like it is picking and choosing where to go."

"You said it's more toxic than VX, so the lethal dose must be incredibly small, right?" The Major was dumbfounded. He had no idea that the ark was so deadly. Why would it even exist? If it truly was created by the ancient Israelites at the behest of God, why would it be necessary? Shouldn't it have been destroyed by now?

"Much smaller doses than VX, believe it or not. It's hard to tell an exact number, testing only on these small animals, but our best guess says that, for the average sized human, five milligrams of vapor touching the skin is lethal within ten seconds. Unfortunately, we have no way of knowing the lethal dose for inhalation, the subject dies before the vapor even enters the lungs."

"Let's just start this demonstration. I want to see it happen." The Major was staring intently at the artifact, floating in the pool of water. It was unnerving to see the monks still standing in the room. They weren't really doing anything, just moving slowly around, talking to themselves, their usual behavior. One of the monks was asleep in his carved out stone bed.

"Commencing animal trial number seventeen," Dr. Kowalski spoke quietly into the small microphone set on the side of his equipment. "There are goggles attached to the underside of each chair in the room. If you want to keep your vision, I suggest that you wear them." Everyone complied at once. The large metal arm at the top of the cavern began to descend toward the ark, slowly and ominously. The animals in the cages were completely oblivious to their fast-approaching doom.

The claw of the mechanical arm grabbed the heavy lid of ark, making a dull thudding sound. Everyone in the room held their breath. "Ready?" Dr. Kowalski asked in a hushed voice, barely able to see the ark through the blacked-out glasses.

"Just hope the water in these walls works. I have no intention of dying today," the Major whispered back. Dr. Kowalski entered a value into his controls and the lid lifted slightly off the ark, for no more than three seconds, and then dropped back to cover the artifact again with a resounding clang.

As soon as the lid fell back into place, Dr. Kowalski started a stopwatch. "Give it at least one minute before you open the door. The monks tell us that as long as the lid is closed, we will never have any sort of problems, but it can't hurt to be too sure." Everyone was on edge, taking their goggles off and replacing them under the chairs. The room was silent, waiting for the minute to be gone. The two rabbits in cages inside the room hopped about nervously in their little prison cells.

"Why did we need the goggles?" the Major asked, looking at Dr. Kowalski for an answer. "I didn't see any flash of light from the ark."

"That's right," the scientist replied, "we don't really know what caused the monks to become blind, the goggles are just another precaution, can't take any risks, right?"

The Major nodded his approval, appreciating the respect that Dr. Kowalski was showing towards the artifact.

"Alright, let's go see the damage." Dr. Kowalski pushed a button on his console, reverting the water sealed door to a functional state, and ushered everyone into the chamber. If the monks in the chamber had noticed that the ark had been opened, they did well not to show it. The animals in the cages were clearly dead. The rabbit closest to the edge of the pool of water had a small line of blood running from its mouth to the ground.

"Their eyes are all dilated, blood pooling in their mouths and skulls, like they suffocated to death in an instant. Weird," the Major said, more to himself than anyone else. It was the first time since Vatican City that he had seen the power of the ark with his own eyes. He lifted one of the rabbits out of its cage, gingerly holding the lifeless body, looking for some clues as to why the ark would even exist. "Have the monks said anything about the origins of the ark? Why would such a device, if made by God, be necessary to existence? This one object is the most efficient and thoroughly destructive weapon of mass destruction ever known to man."

The scientists in the room stopped what they were doing and just looked at the Major, taken aback by the unexpected moment of profundity. "The better question," Dr. Kowalski said softly, "is that if such a thing exists, why would God, an all powerful being, allow it to be here in this room right now, in your hands?" He didn't say it with any anger or spite, just plain curiosity. The weight of the question hanging in the room was palpable.

"*Our* hands," the Major corrected, letting the dead rabbit slide from his grasp and back into its cage. "Why would God let this wonderful weapon remain in *our* hands?" The Major paused, letting everything sink in, mulling his words over in his head before speaking them. "There can be only one logical answer. Either this so-called Ark of the Covenant was made by the hands of men and there is no God, or else God is not intrinsically morally good."

"Yes," Dr. Kowalski started to respond, being well versed in philosophy and enjoying the mental experiment, "by the very definition of God, He is a being of unsurpassed good matched with limitless power. By that logic, any action He does not directly prevent, because He has the power to do so, means that God Himself is purposely willing it to happen."

"So what does that make us?" the Major asked, looking Dr. Kowalski in the eyes. "If this God of yours has the power to control every single event in the entire universe with but a thought and chooses to let us take control of one of the most holy relics of the first Israelites and watches as we massacre cities with it, what are we?" The Major smiled, seeing his argument unfold in his head and liking it. "Messengers of God, carrying out the Lord's divine will through the mere fact that our actions are not stopped? Or has God given up on us, on humanity, and wishes to see it purged? Is the ark simply another method of flooding the earth and starting over?"

Everyone had been thinking those same thoughts for weeks. Perhaps not as eloquently as the Major and Dr. Kowalski, but all of the scientists working on the mysteries of the ark knew that it was intended as a weapon, and they had stayed, fighting their own moral struggles. Perhaps it was fear that kept them coming to work each day, afraid that if they left the project, they would be hunted down and killed to protect the secret, or perhaps it was just the natural quest for knowledge that exists within every being of higher intelligence.

"Look, when I agreed to open the ark at Vatican City, it was for the purpose of research. All of the early sources, the most reliable sources, point towards God directing the killing energies of the ark to purge the unclean from this world. Opening the Ark of the Covenant on Easter Sunday underneath Saint Peter's Square seemed like the most foolproof way to test that theory." The scientists nodded as Dr. Kowalski spoke, everyone looking at the Major.

"As far as we know, the kid you let escape was the only one who survived. Maybe that was on purpose, maybe God spared him specifically, but I doubt it. That kid got lucky, that's all there is to it." Dr. Kowalski moved to the door as he spoke, starting to ascend back to the laboratory.

"Is that it?" the Major called after him. "Your noble and self-righteous plan to cleanse the world of sin and vice either failed or would involve the slaughter of all of humanity to achieve so you just walk away? Does your moral conscience not require you to kill me and seal the ark forever? How do you justify it to yourself? How will you sleep in Argentina, knowing that I have the ark, knowing that I'll open it again, in another city, maybe even open it under your house in Buenos Aires? Tell me that." The Major was at the top of the staircase, right behind his oldest friends.

"Because I still have hope. Hope that you will do the right thing, that your salvation will be at hand. Those questions? How will I sleep at night? Ask yourself the same things." Dr. Kowalski left the Major there stunned, standing awkwardly speechless in the doorway.

The Major just stood there and watched, nervously rubbing the handle of his familiar pistol, as Dr. Kowalski and his team of scientists cleaned out their offices and left, supposedly headed for asylum in Argentina.

Chapter 13

I walked slowly up to the street level, trying to get my bearings. I tossed the lab coat into a trash can as I exited the garage into the night. My own winter jacket kept me warm, but not warm enough, winter had set in. How long had I been like that, handcuffed to a hospital bed? There was a crisp layer of frost on the cold concrete of the sidewalk. I tried to remain calm and inconspicuous but the cold night air kept setting my teeth to chattering.

As soon as I was out of sight of the hospital I started to run. Blood was pumping out of the bandage around my neck with every step but I couldn't stop. Fear and the cold kept me running back towards the ghetto and the abandoned neighborhood I called my home. I had to get to the rest of the group, get the recording we had made, and end this, once and for all.

Out of breath and with blood flowing freely down my torn neck, I saw the entrance to the neighborhood, the overgrown stone wall at the beginning of the street. I ran harder, looking right at the house, hoping to see someone I knew, hoping that they weren't dead. I stopped on the street, standing before the house. Police tape was surrounding the entire property. My heart sank. I sat down on the street, feeling faint. I grabbed at the back of my neck, trying to stem the flow of blood, feeling the soaked bandage starting to fall off of my skin, too saturated to be of any use. I sat there on the cold pavement, my heart racing, trying to think of what to do next.

The cold, it was just so cold. Snow was starting to fall silently around me, coating me in a layer of icy frost. My metal arm was freezing inside the coat sleeve. I started to cry, the warm tears stinging my cold face. Running was no longer even a thought in my mind. I curled up into a ball, trying to stay warm, feeling the blood from neck pooling around me on the ground, mixing with the snow to form a gruesome, bloody sleet. I thought back to Red and Abigail, thinking of how accepting and nice they had been, taking me in off the street, knowing nothing about me, and trusting me simply because I was honest with them. I closed my eyes, the cold and blood loss beginning to take their toll.

"Look here, Red, he came back," I could hear Abigail whisper in my head, imagining her hands reaching down to touch me on the shoulder.

"I thought for sure they would've killed him. Judging by all this blood, it looks like they did try." It was Red. I could hear him speaking in my head, the delusion seemed almost real. I could feel his hands on my back, lifting me off the cold ground. Imagining them was comforting, making me feel warm inside. My teeth stopped chattering and I simply laid there, still.

"His skin is turning blue, he lost a lot of blood, Red," her voice sounded so real, so close. I imagined her standing behind me, bundled up, a look of honest concern on her face as I lay limp in Red's strong arms.

"We need to take him to Dime, he will know what to do. We need to get him there quickly, I don't think he will last much longer." Red was smiling in my mind as he spoke the words, looking down on me like a father. I could feel my consciousness slipping away, like it was being pulled by some ghostly hands, wrenched out of my head. I tried to open my eyes, to keep my sanity, to at least greet my icy death with a smile on my face, not shivering in my sleep like a baby animal that won't make it through winter. Everything was just dark and cold, so cold.

"Father," I could hear a disembodied voice saying. It sounded like me, from when I was a kid, looking at my own father, dressed in his military fatigues, going off to war. It was the last time I had ever seen him. The voice wasn't mine though, and it wasn't a memory, I could tell. The voice was coming from my left, from a thousand miles away.

"Son," I heard. It was Red's reassuring voice, the steadiness that years of experience can bring to even the most traumatic situations. He was standing over me. I struggled to open my eyes, without success.

"He will live," I heard the first voice saying, seeming much closer now. I felt a hand on my shoulder, warm and calloused, a man's hand. I wasn't wearing a shirt, I realized. It was warm, my whole body was warm. I could feel a fire burning in the room, probably somewhere near my feet. I tried to move my left arm, to scratch the undying itch on the back of my neck. Someone was holding my hand, Abigail, it must have been Abigail. I managed to twitch my hand, causing the room to hush. I saw my friends in my head, standing in the room, looking at my body. They were bathed in a soft white light in my mind, like angels.

My right arm was still attached, I could sense it. I sent what remained of my consciousness whirling along those familiar pathways of my brain to the artificial nerves inside my skull, activating them as fast as I could. The jolt of pain through my head was so familiar and comforting that it made me smile. I could hear the people in the room standing about me, clapping and patting each other on the back. So, I thought to myself, they didn't expect me to live. I did live, that was a relief.

I clenched the metal fingers of my right hand, taking full control over the prosthetic. The arm moved upwards at my behest, searching for something to grab onto in the air. A hand met it and held on firmly. I used the strength of the prosthetic to pull myself up to a sitting position, my mind a swamp of dizziness.

"Congratulations," Abigail said, squeezing my hand, "you've come back from the dead." I finally opened my eyes. It was a glorious sight, everyone standing around me, a fire burning in an old stove a few feet from my head. The fire was the only light source in the small room. Although the area was warm, I could tell from the condensation on the metal walls that the cold of winter wasn't far away.

"Are we in a storage container?" I asked, indicating with my head the corrugated pattern on the metal walls and the low metal ceiling.

"A shipping container," Dime corrected. "Welcome to my home. I hope you have enjoyed the only bed, I had to sleep on the floor last night." Everyone laughed at that. I even managed a strained chuckle. Red was standing to my right, holding my hand to steady me. Abigail was kneeling by my side, holding my other hand and fighting back tears. The twins were standing next to the old stove, warming their hands over the fire. The stove was connected to a set of old brown pipes that ran in a square around the length of the ceiling before exiting through a hole in the metal roof.

"Frank and Ivan are outside, trying to find us something to eat," Red said, noting the confusion on my face at their absence.

"Thanks for saving me," I managed to say through the grogginess. I noticed the empty syringe of sweet dreams on the floor next to my bed and understood the cause of my paralysis. I used my metal arm to push myself all the way up, resting my back against the cardboard that insulated the wall from the elements. The pain in my back from the gun shot was still tremendous but my neck felt better.

I gingerly reached my arm up, feeling the effects of the drugs slowly leaving my body, and felt the staples. There was a small, L shaped line of six staples holding the flap of skin down tight to my neck. It stung when I moved my head, but other than that, it was a wound I would soon forget.

Frank and Ivan came back in then, the wind howling when they opened the door. They each had two large white plastic bags filled with food. "Hey, you're awake!" Ivan said with a smile. "I knew we were right, getting a meal for you too." The two men set the bags of food down on an old ironing board that served as the only table.

"Sorry, we spent some of your money, Esau," Frank said, handing the containers of Chinese carryout to everyone. It felt like Christmas with the cold wind outside, Frank and Ivan handing out food as though they themselves were Santa Claus. Everyone ate their food in contented silence. My neck and back hurt with every bite, but it was good to have some warm food after the crushing cold of the previous night.

Abigail was the first to speak when the chicken and fried rice was all gone. "So," she said, looking from Red to me, "what do we do now? We can't stay here forever. I'm sure that the police know where this place is. It's only a matter of time before they bust that door down and shoot us all." It was a good question, one that no one wanted to think about. We were truly homeless now, without even a shelter to call our home. The police would be on high alert, monitoring everything, at every moment.

"We need to finish this. We just need to show our hand, make our play, and hope for the best. I think we can all agree that our time has run out. This is the only option." Surprisingly, it was Frank, not Red or Abigail, who began outlining a plan. Luckily, Abigail had grabbed the recording from the safe after she fled the house. We didn't have much to go on, but we had something. That little recorder was our only source of hope.

"What can you do to help us, Jericho?" Red asked his son, sounding desperate.

"Well," Dime said, waving his hands around the room, "what you see is what I have. Everything is yours. I know it's not much, but it's yours." To say that Dime had 'not much' in the way of supplies was an overstatement. He had nothing. There were stacks of old books along the walls but other than the heater and the bed, there was nothing.

"Jericho," Red stared him in the eyes as he spoke, "we need supplies, something real. You need to come through. Can you get us some stuff by tomorrow?" Dime sighed, not looking at anything but the floor.

"It will take every favor I'm owed, and then some, to get anything for you guys. The cops have the whole ghetto on lock down," Dime said, looking and sounding desperate.

"Just get what you can. It wouldn't surprise me if this thing turns into an all out war between us and the heavily armed and armored cops. We need you now, Jericho," Red pointed towards the door. "Go, don't come back without something useful." Red spoke the words with such a finality that Dime simply stood, put on a coat, and walked out into the cold teeth of winter.

We spent the entire day trying to figure out a plan. In the end, I was the only one who wanted to just go to the police with the evidence we had and try our luck. Everyone else considered it suicide. My mind and body were too battered to come up with any useful plan.

Luckily, Dime came back the next morning with good news. He had scouted out the laboratory and reported that everyone was leaving, abandoning the facility it seemed. Dime had used some of his old prison contacts to get us a few allies. He had people meeting at the old bookstore the next morning, ready to help us in any way they could.

He brought a large military style duffle bag filled with supplies. Somehow he was able to get his hands on a number of guns, plenty of ammunition, ropes, a grappling hook, and enough knives for us each to take two. No one asked where he got the materials but we all looked a bit curious at the sight of a pack of six military smoke grenades. At least, we assumed they were smoke grenades, the package was printed in German so we were really just guessing.

"How on earth do German military grenades make it all the way to the United States undetected?" I mumbled, rummaging through the supplies.

"The black market is a wonderful thing," Dime replied, handing me a gun. "Anything you can imagine, anything at all, you can find it. You just have to know the right people, of course."

We still had three vials of sweet dreams left over so our plan began to come together quite simply. An ambush would be set, using me as the bait, at our old bench in the ghetto. We would wait for the police to notice me and then for them to call the Major in. When the Major got there, we wouldn't have much time to act. We all knew that he would shoot first and ask questions later.

The eight of us waited near the old used bookstore, hoping to see a large crowd form in our support. The army of the homeless started to show up around dawn.

The first to arrive was some sort of hardcore biker gang, by the looks of them. Twelve of the burliest men I had ever seen pulled up in front of the bookstore and waited, leaning against the wall. Their motorcycles all had large American flags waving from the back, creating a very intimidating albeit patriotic scene. Dime explained that they were from the local chapter of some sort of society that follows a certain death metal band around.

More and more people showed up, in pairs or by themselves for the next few hours. We waited until almost noon before Dime rallied the troops and got everyone organized. We deployed our new army in a parking lot not far from the old bench where Red and the rest of us used to live. We had two score of soldiers, all told. Apparently, when the police are going to war against the homeless ghetto dwellers, the downtrodden organize quickly and are eager for a fight.

Our commanders, Abigail and Dime, went over our makeshift plan with everyone and got into position. I, the best bait we had, simply stood, milling about the area where I first met Red. Red himself sat on the bench with Ivan, leaving Frank and the twins to sit off to the side, pretending to be asleep against the side of a building. Our new additions hid in strategic places all around the street, setting the ambush perfectly.

It didn't take long for the first police car to roll by, clearly seeing me. I had to fight off the urge to sarcastically wave to the police cruiser when it passed. Within ten minutes of the first black and white car passing by, five police cars pulled up, lights flashing, sirens blaring. Behind them all was a black town car with tinted windows, most likely containing the Major, his signature pistol at the ready.

Right on cue, the bikers sped around the corner, flags unfurled, racing in between all of police cars, creating a visual barrier. I leapt behind the bench, crouching, hiding myself for a moment.

Just as we all expected, the police started to open fire, shooting wildly at the bikers, shattering the peaceful serenity of the winter day. I felt the wind from one shot soaring above my head, almost killing me right there and spilling my brains all over the pavement. Less than a second later another shot thudded into the hard concrete of the bench, sending shrapnel exploding upwards. Luckily for me, it didn't penetrate the bench and find my gut.

The rest of Dime's army came roaring around the corner opposite of the bikers, tackling the Major's cronies, taking down the ones close enough to fire at me, raining blows down upon them with makeshift clubs. I could see two officers moving up from the cars in the back, weapons drawn and waiting for an open shot to take me down. I braced my shoulder against the hard concrete of the bench, squarely positioning my feet underneath my chest and lifting with all of my might, using my considerable strength to unseat the bench from the ground.

I came forward in a rush, launching the concrete bench into the torsos of the two nearest officers, taking them to the ground in an instant. One of them managed to get a shot off right as I threw the bench, sending another spray of concrete chips into the air. I quickly jumped the bench and moved to the nearest police car, ducking down and sliding, using the front of the car as a barrier. I could feel the surgery scars on my chest sliding and pulling with every movement. Images of the scars being ripped open ran through my head, threatening to destroy my will.

Glancing to my right with my back against the hood of the car I saw Abigail, engaged with an officer, wrestling him to the ground with a knife in her hand. Another officer came around from the car nearest to Abigail, his weapon drawn. Without even thinking, I grabbed the pistol from my waistline and fired, hitting the policeman solidly in the chest, sending him sprawling backwards. Abigail looked back over her shoulder, smiling at me through the blood covering her face.

She tossed me a short length of black nylon rope before turning and running, finding her next target within the chaos. I could hear the voice of the Major, somewhere behind me, shouting, calling for my blood. I reached my hand around the corner of the car I was using as a barrier and wrenched a chunk of old pavement free. Bullets were ricocheting everywhere in a maelstrom of fury as I opened the door to the police car and leaned inside. I tied the rope to the steering wheel, connecting the other end to the passenger-side door and dropped the rock on the accelerator, turning the key in the ignition.

I smiled as I rolled out, hitting the ground as the car took off. It turned a tight circle, hitting two cars behind it and taking out the officers nearby. I saw the Major then. He was standing behind two policemen in riot gear, holding bulletproof shields. The Major stood there like a monolith of power, expressionless in his black Kevlar vest. I could see his signature pearl-handled revolver clenched tightly in his fist, pointed right at me. I lurched to the side, anticipating the shot, and got caught by a hail of smoking pavement as the bullet hit the spot where I had just been crouched.

I fired a few shots back, squeezing the trigger in rapid succession, knowing I wouldn't hit him at that distance, but wanting to at least buy some time. With my head turned, running for cover, I heard the shots hit one of the riot shields, hopefully staggering the man holding it enough to knock him into the Major, unbalancing his next shot. I got lucky, I was right. The second shot from the revolver went far wide, missing me by a few feet and digging into the ground.

I kept low to the ground, altering my course as much as I could, creating a random trail that I hoped would cause the Major to miss. Two bikers in leather jackets came at me then, riding hard. They split, going wide around me, one to either side, and I used the visual obstruction to cut hard to my left, heading for the spot where Ivan and Frank were hiding behind a building.

I motioned to Frank, giving him a 'thumbs up', our signal for a grenade. He tossed one of the small black objects to me and I wasted no time pulling the pin and lobbing it behind my back. We had been wrong, they weren't smoke grenades.

A violent shock ripped through the air and everything went silent. I fell to the ground from the force of the explosion at my back. I struggled to regain my wits, everything in my mind was scrambled beyond sense. I could see Frank and Ivan in front of me, clutching their eyes and writhing around the ground in pain. My head was so boggled that it was all I could do to clamber to my knees and crawl forward.

Just as quickly as we had all been knocked to the ground and disoriented, the effects faded. My hearing returned and my thoughts cleared as I got up into a run and made it to the edge of the building, standing next to Frank and Ivan.

"Wow," I said, breathing heavily, "those things are intense. I have an idea, give me another." Frank handed me a second grenade and I bolted back around the corner, into the fray once more.

I was looking for Abigail but I couldn't find her. The bikers were causing so much chaos and blocking my view that it was nearly impossible to tell what was even going on. One of the twins caught my eye, running towards me at a sprint. She was bleeding from her chest but it didn't look incredibly serious. She had a knife tucked under her belt at her side.

I passed her in full stride, taking the knife from her as I went. The Major emerged then, about twenty paces or so ahead of me, still flanked by his heavily armored guards. It was little consolation to note the many dings and blemishes on the shields.

I launched the knife at the Major, aiming high and not really sure how to throw a knife with any accuracy or effect. Just as I hoped, the riot shields both went up, blocking the knife with ease. What they didn't notice was the grenade I had rolled under their shields when they went high. I launched myself as far as I could, back in the direction of the corner of the building I had come from. The explosion ripped through the air again, although not nearly as violently as before.

I smiled to myself, imagining the chaos I had caused, hoping the sturdy riot shields had absorbed and concentrated the blast, completely annihilating the Major's sensory perceptions.

Scrambling to my feet, I managed to look back over my shoulder. The two officers were down, clearly stunned. I couldn't see the Major but I knew he had to have taken a brutal shock from the grenade. I raced back to the fallen officers, looking for the Major. The two armored guards were starting to stir and going for their weapons, something I could not allow. I planted a foot on the nearest man's shield, pinning him under it while I grabbed the gun from the second man, beating him to it by a few inches. It was a taser on his side, not a pistol. Reaching down and hitting the man hard across the jaw with my metallic arm and sending him back to the ground, I used my other arm to press the end of the taser against his leg. Hoping that it wouldn't be as heavily armored as the rest of him, I pulled the trigger.

The officer convulsed violently on the ground underneath me and I knew he was done. I lifted my foot off the shield of the first man and hit him on the top of the head with my fist, sending his thoughts to the swirling abyss of unconsciousness. I lifted the shield off his arm and stood, surveying the wreckage, looking for any sign of the Major.

Abigail caught up to my side, taking the second shield from the wounded man and grinning, covered in blood that most likely was not hers. "There he goes," she bellowed, yelling and pointing at the Major. The man was running, his back turned like a beaten dog, and heading for the black car that brought him here. I charged ahead, the shield on my left arm leading the way.

The lithe and dexterous woman looted the unused taser from the downed officer and followed in close pursuit. The Major, dazed from the grenade, couldn't move as quickly as the two of us. I caught up to him right as he reached for the car door and body-slammed him into it, hitting him with the full force of the shield and crushing his body against the metal frame of the vehicle. Abigail stood behind me, taser at the ready, waiting for a clear shot to bring him down. I looked into the man's face for the first time, seeing true fear behind his crystalline blue eyes. Balling my metal hand into a heavy fist, I brought the full force of my arm to bear against the top of the car frame, inches from the Major's head, a move designed to send enough fear into the Major to cause him to surrender. The car frame collapsed under the weight of the blow, breaking the glass in both of the doors on that side of the car.

"Mankind is a festering parasite," the Major growled, barely audible from the other side of the riot shield. I pulled back a few inches and slammed him again, sending blood splattering from his nose all over the shield. The Major started to push back against the shield, grinning and howling like some sort of primal beast, bloodlust filling his eyes.

I heard the crash of the cars before I felt it, a sharp burst of metal crumpling against metal, screeching and piercing.

The police car I had set into motion earlier slammed into the front quarter panel of the Major's car, knocking the side view mirror into my prisoner's side and sending him sprawling to the pavement. The front of the car continued to skid forward, hitting me full in the legs and knocking me to the ground. I had to scramble to avoid being crushed under the tires.

I heard Abigail shriek behind me, pulling the trigger on the taser. "Damn," she yelled, missing the Major with the weapon. I got to my feet, pain shooting through my left knee, and tossed the shield to the ground, not wanting the weight to slow me down. The two of us took off after the Major.

He was running down the middle of the street, passed the wreckage of cars, motorcycles, and people. I couldn't keep up with the wound to my knee; I knew the Major would get away. I searched the carnage for a motorcycle that looked functional. I found one that looked promising, pulling the large biker out from under it and standing it upright. "How do I start this thing?" I yelled to the fallen biker before I realized that he was dead, shot through the heart.

Abigail rushed up to my side, "let me do it," she barked, hitting the starter and causing the bike to roar to life, "twist the handle back to accelerate," she said, making the motion with her hand.

"I know that much," I called back over my shoulder as I sped away. It was the first time I had ever ridden a motorcycle and I was clearly terrible at it. I watched the Major running away, gaining distance as I struggled to keep the bike upright on the broken pavement. "I can't drive this thing," I yelled back to Abigail, my heart sinking as I watched the Major getting away. I turned the bike over on its side, motioning for Abigail to drive.

She hopped onto the bike in front of me, kicking it into motion and sending us speeding down the street. I reached my arms around her and held on with all my strength, terrified. We zoomed around the wreckage of a police car and ramped over a fallen motorcycle, soaring through the air in some of the most terrifying moments of my life. In just a few seconds we were almost upon the Major, still running through the center of the street. He glanced back to see our approach, fear in his cold eyes, steam rising from the heat of his sweat.

The Major cut hard to his right, turning onto the sidewalk, putting street lights and fire hydrants in our path. "Hold on," Abigail said over her shoulder, ripping the accelerator as hard as she could. I closed my eyes and strengthened my grip, praying not to die.

Much to my enjoyment, I did not die. Abigail was a very skilled driver. She hit the gas, lurching the bike forward, sending it over the edge of the sidewalk in front of the Major's path. I have no idea how, but she was able to set the bike down on its front wheel at the same time she turned, sending the back wheel high into the air and nearly dumping the two of us over the handlebars. I grit my teeth and expected to hit the ground, crushed beneath the bike. The back wheel connected with something solid, hitting it hard. A gasp told me it was the Major's chest, his ribs snapping like wet twigs. Abigail leapt from the bike, forcing me to do the same. The Major hit the ground hard, all the air missing from his battered chest and lungs.

Abigail was quick to pin him to the ground, her fist taking the front teeth from the Major's mouth in a violent spray of blood. She pulled a syringe of sweet dreams from her belt and slammed it down hard into the Major's shoulder, injecting him with the potent liquid. I smiled as the Major's eyes went dim, the fight fading from his cold limbs.

Abigail and I dragged the Major's limp body back to the bench area, the remaining police having fled after the retreat of their commander. "Is anyone hurt?" I asked when we returned, a question I instantly regretted asking once I looked around at the mess.

"Maria is," Red said, leaning over her with a strip of cloth. There were many wounded scattered all about. Abigail and I tossed the Major down onto the hood of one of the disabled police cars and went straight to Maria's side. She was bleeding pretty badly from the center of her chest.

"What happened to her? Did you see it?" Abigail asked, clutching her hand.

"Well, I didn't see anything myself, but I pulled two taser leads out of her thigh. Looks like they shot her once she went down, hit her right in the chest, just below the breastbone." It was grave news. Judging by the ashen look on Maria's face, she wasn't going to last long.

"Dime, get over here," Red called to his son, "you know how to fix people better than any of us." Dime was tending his own wound, a vicious looking slice on his right shoulder. His face was battered and bruised and he moved with a noticeable limp. Still, he came as fast as he could to tend to Maria.

Dime lifted her off the ground slightly, feeling with his hand under her body for an exit wound. "The bullet didn't come out. We need to get it before it kills her." We all knew what had to be done but none of us wanted to do it.

"Will she live, if you can get the bullet out in time?" It was Mary. She was uninjured but looked as though she would die standing up in front of us.

"I don't think so," Dime replied quietly, causing Mary to fall to her knees, wailing for her twin sister. "Esau, bring me my multi-tool, from the bag. I stashed it around the corner, by Frank with the grenades." I ran to get the bag as quickly as I could, knowing that every moment of delay would be one more moment for Maria to die.

I tossed the tool to Dime and he began to cut off Maria's shirt, inspecting the wound. It was bad. Every ragged breath that she took caused more dark blood to bubble up from the wound and roll down her sides.

"Alright, I'm not exactly sure what I'm doing here, but I know we need to get the bullet out." Dime folded the multi-tool, inserting the pliers end into the bullet hole. Mary was crying hard at her sister's side, one hand holding Maria's hand, one hand clutching the front of Abigail's shirt for support.

"I can't watch this, man," Red said, turning away as the blood began to flow freely down the young woman's ashen body.

"Then go," I told him, "see if anyone else is seriously wounded, help them. And bring some water for Maria."

Red left without a word, not being able to stomach the carnage of the battlefield surgery.

Dime had the pliers fully inserted into the wound, feeling around for the bullet. Maria was starting to cough, barely conscious, her eyes rolling back into her head.

"I can't find it," Dime said in desperation, blood covering his hand. He pulled the pliers out, quickly covering the bullet hole with his hand, trying to keep the woman from bleeding out right there on the hard pavement.

"Let me try," I said, moving closer to Maria's side. I don't know what made me say it, I just felt like I had to at least try. I couldn't just sit there and watch as one of my friends died, doing nothing to save her. Dime handed me the pliers and I used them much like I used the scissors on the back of my neck in the hospital room, inserting them into the wound and opening, using it to widen the area and get a better view.

I had no idea what I was really looking at, other than blood. Dime grabbed a flashlight from his bag and shone it into the wound. I had to cover my mouth to keep from coughing and retching. The sight of a human being's innards, wounded and covered in blood, made my stomach churn no matter how focused I was on saving the life in front of me.

Red came back with a bottle of water and half-full bottle of vodka. I took the water and tossed it on the wound, trying to clear away some of the blood so I could see, looking for the bullet. "I think that's the liver," I said, looking at a pale reddish organ with a tear in it, marking the path of the bullet.

Remembering a few Civil War documentaries I had seen, I grabbed the bottle of vodka from Red, taking a healthy swig for myself before splashing some onto the wound, disinfecting it. Maria was barely conscious, moaning softly as I poured the vodka into the wound.

"Vodka directly onto the liver? Is that going to make her drunk?" It was a good question, one I hadn't thought of. If it did, it wouldn't hurt. Assuming Maria lived, she wouldn't want to remember this ordeal anyways.

"No idea," I told Abigail with a shrug, not sure what to say.

Dime continued to shine the flashlight into the wound and I pushed the pliers in further, attempting to open the tear in the liver and hoping to see the bullet. The light reflected off a piece of metal, glinting for a moment. We found it! I held the liver open with my left hand, blood making everything almost too slick to work, and I sent my right hand into Maria's chest, feeling the metal of the bullet touching the metal of my fingertips.

It took all of my concentration to pinch the edge of the bullet between two of my fingers and gingerly pull it out. "Get something in her mouth for her to bite, I'm betting this will hurt like nothing she has ever felt before," I told Abigail who promptly ripped a sleeve off of her shirt and twisted it before placing it between Maria's teeth.

I was right. Maria, still barely conscious, felt the bullet exiting her liver keenly. She screamed, arching hurt back, throwing blood all over the pavement and my hands. Her body convulsed as I removed the bullet, her back being wracked by spasms.

"Can't we just give her some of the sweet dreams?" Abigail asked through her tears, hoping to find some way to comfort her writhing sister.

"I'm afraid that if we do, she won't be strong enough to wake up," I replied, dropping the bullet into my palm. I truly didn't know if the drug would hurt or help her but it wasn't worth the risk.

I opened my palm to show Maria's twin the bullet, trying to give her some consolation and assure her that Maria would live but as soon as I opened my hand I knew we weren't finished. "It's only half there," I whispered, not believing it. The bullet had fragmented in Maria's liver. Or perhaps the rest of it was somewhere else, lodged in her diaphragm, her spleen, maybe even her heart or lungs. It could be anywhere.

I sat back, not wanting to see the bleeding woman or the bullet anymore, wishing it would all just go away. "Look," Dime said, inspecting the bullet, "it split almost perfectly in half. I bet the front half is right by the spot where you took out the back half."

I glanced again at the bloody bullet, realizing that Dime was speaking the truth. If the bullet broke into a front and a back half, logic would dictate that the front half wouldn't be far from the back. The bullet was broken clean through the center, an odd fragmentation.

"You have to get it, Dime, get the second the half," I said, not having the willpower to put my hands back into the bloody liver of my near-death friend. Abigail took the flashlight and held it for Dime as he opened the wound again.

I could hear Maria's muffled screams as the two worked to retrieve the fragment. I laid down on the pavement, physically and emotionally exhausted from the battle and the surgery, not wanting to be part of the world any more. I only glanced back once at the body of the Major, just to make sure he hadn't arisen by some miracle from his drug induced slumber and stalked off while no one was paying any attention to him.

The satisfaction of seeing the Major lying there on the hood of the car, unconscious, was indeed great. It would have brought a smile to my face to see him like that, if it weren't for Maria lying on the ground, about to die. I looked up at the sky as I sat there, listening to the muffled cries of my dying friend, the violent sobs and shakes of her twin sister, and the quietly comforting words of Abigail, all while thinking to myself, how could such evil exist? How could that man, lying limp behind me, possess within himself such capacity for evil that would allow him to slaughter an entire city and then wage all-out war against me in order to keep it a secret? Why?

Needless to say, I was looking forward to beating some answers out of the Major. It was about time that he explained everything. Torturing him would only be an added to bonus to the satisfaction of ending the Major's plans.

"Finally," Dime said under his breath, "got the second piece." The screaming had stopped. Everything was quiet when Dime turned around to show everyone the second fragment of the bullet in his tattooed hand. Maria wasn't moving on the ground. She was just lying there, completely still. Her skin was so pale, matching the snow that was drifting down around her. I knew before I got up to see her that she was dead. The trauma had been too much for her small body to handle.

Before any of us knew what was happening, Mary had stood up, a knife in her hand. She charged past me at full speed, howling at the top of her lungs, tears streaming down her face. I wasn't sure what she was going to do, until I saw her looking right at the Major, death in her pretty blue eyes.

I stood, trying to catch the back of Mary's jacket, my arm reaching out but only touching air as she ran by. Leaping, she came down hard upon the Major's chest, knife point leading the way.

"No!" I called out, not wanting our best piece of evidence and the source of all of our answers to die before explaining everything.

The knife sunk in to the hilt, right through the ribs, directly over the Major's heart. Blood spurted forth from the deep puncture wound as Mary pulled her arm up, jerking the knife free and going for a second stab. His throat was next to go, the knife taking his Adam's apple and throwing it onto the ground like litter. The blood continued to flow, cascading in waves down the Major's chest and staining the white hood of the police car a deep crimson.

I was at Mary's side by then, intent on restraining her. Red was there too, just watching. I looked to him but he only shrugged, desperation stamped clearly on his face. We both stood there, watching Mary hack apart the torn corpse of the Major, the man who caused the brutal death of her twin sister.

The knife broke a few minutes into the carnal massacre, the blade stuck deep into the Major's groin. Much to our surprise, Mary continued to bludgeon the gory mess of a body, slugging away with the heavy metal handle of the knife, sending teeth, blood and bits of broken skull all over the ground and everything nearby.

She finally collapsed, exhausted and crying, falling to the ground on her knees in the pool of blood she created. The carnage that she left behind was almost unrecognizable as human. Thinking back to all those bodies strewn about Saint Peter's Square, the little girl I had used to hide my own body, the blood that had dropped out of her mouth and onto my skin, thinking of all that almost made the corpse of the Major seem like somehow his punishment wasn't enough, that nothing could ever be enough to atone for what he had done.

"Come on," Red said, surveying the entire area, "more police will be here soon enough, likely with plenty of armored backup. They will want us dead for what happened here, especially when they see that." He nodded towards the mess on the hood of the police car in front of Mary. It was true, I knew. I just couldn't find the energy to put my legs in motion and leave. Where would we go? None of us knew. The house was out of the question, they would surely have it under constant surveillance.

The biker gang had left right after the fighting quieted, taking their two dead with them and salvaging the best of the destroyed motorcycles. The other homeless that Dime had rallied to our cause had dispersed, none of them wanting to witness a surgery taking place with a multi-tool and flashlight on the cold concrete.

We salvaged what we could from the battlefield, taking what useful things we found. Not having the supplies to make a proper stretcher to carry Maria, we used the military duffle bag that Dime had brought with the straps slung between Abigail and I to carry Maria's body away. We didn't know exactly where we were going, we just walked. No one spoke much until we arrived at one of the many small parks that dotted the downtown area of the city.

Epilogue

It was still early enough in the day that the few people we did see on the streets didn't bother us at all, even seeing the body being carried by our group. The park had a few small streams with quaint wooden bridges decorated in a beautiful Japanese décor.

It seemed like a fitting place to bury our friend. The pond at the center of the park had a grassy area underneath a cherry blossom tree. The pink petals of the tree drifted slowly to the ground, mixing with the light snow. The bridge leading to the island was flanked by two carved wooden poles, each bearing the words of 'peace' in all the languages of the world. We carried Maria's body to the island, resting it gently under the colorful boughs of the wide tree. There was no one else in the park and the soft crunching of frost under our feet created an eerily peaceful atmosphere.

It was tough to dig the grave with the ground being so cold and almost frozen. We had no shovel so all of us got down on our hands and knees and tore up great chunks of earth with our hands. Doing that labor ourselves, feeling the pain in our fingers as we created our friend's final resting place brought some sort of closure to us. It didn't take much longer than an hour to dig a sizeable grave, using the strength of my arm to speed up the excavation.

We set Maria in the ground as gently as we could, trying to make her look peaceful, like she was simply asleep. It was hard to think of her that way, seeing her chest covered in blood, the cut-up shirt barely disguising her wounds. Abigail bent down and crossed Maria's arms over her chest, doing what she could to hide the blood and gore.

We scooped the dirt back into the hole, slowly burying our fallen friend. The sun was high in the sky by the time it was done. The seven of us stood there in a circle around the fresh grave, all just waiting for someone to say something appropriate.

"Well," Abigail started, "she was a good sister. She will be missed dearly." Abigail and Mary were both crying silently, holding each other for support.

Red was next to speak, his soft voice rumbling through the falling snow. "We commend our sister Maria to the peaceful meadows of heaven. May her death not be in vain and may her life always serve as an inspiration to those she left behind, directing us toward the good and true." It was the best eulogy that we were likely to hear. We stood there a few moments longer, saying our own goodbyes in our minds. Mary never said a word during the impromptu service. She simply stood there next to the fresh grave of her twin and looked at the dirt longingly.

We left the grave in silence, walking, but without any real purpose. "We can't go back to the house," Ivan said once we were out of the park." Everyone nodded in agreement.

"Esau, you and I have to get out of these bloody clothes. The two of us are dead giveaways," Dime said sullenly, opening the duffle bag and producing two clean shirts. We stood at the exit of the park, trying to clean the blood off of our bodies so that we could pass unnoticed on the streets.

The cut on Dime's shoulder was bleeding, marring the beautiful tattoo covering his back. I couldn't help but watch as the thin line of blood trickled down the branches of Yggdrasil, marvelously tattooed into the man's skin. There were four stags and a dragon intertwined with the roots around Dime's waistline, branches displaying all of the seasons reaching from the top of his back to the base of his skull. It was mesmerizing, the way the branches changed from buds to blooming leaves and then to barren branches. The cut on Dime's shoulder split the sacred tree down the side, cleaving some of the branches away.

"We should probably leave town," Red replied sullenly as Dime pulled a new shirt over his head. "Anyone have any ideas? Where do we go?" No one spoke for a long time. We passed a police car after only a few minutes of walking out of the park, its lights flashing, but it simply sped right past us without notice. No one so much as flinched when it zoomed by, everyone deeply absorbed in their own thoughts.

"Well," I said, "we are headed south right now. I say we just keep going. We still have a few guns left, we can sell all but one of them and use the money to buy some food along our way." It was as good of a plan as I could come up with.

Abigail, walking right beside me, slipped her hand inside mine. "Sounds good to me," she said. "We can make it out of the city by nightfall if we keep going this way."

"We still have the recording," Ivan added, "we can try taking it to a police department in another city and see if they will believe us." We all just shrugged, not knowing if they would even listen to our story or not, and trudged on.

We left the city right as the sun dipped below the horizon, a fresh layer of frost crunching beneath our feet. Our little group headed southwest, our pockets filled with money from the firearms that Dime was able to sell on the street. No plan, no direction, no real purpose, we simply walked out of the city, out of our home, in search of a new place to live.

The seven monks gathered around the small pool in the basement of Schwartz Laboratories, looking to their leader for direction. "We are again tasked with the concealment of the Ark of the Covenant, like we have done so many times before," their leader said. The monks bowed their heads, a sign of agreement and obedience.

"Where shall we take it?" one of the younger monks asked, his blind eyes staring at their leader.

"The Mount Hor location has been compromised," their leader responded. He was holding the blank book from the podium in his hands, leafing through its crinkled and withered pages.

"How many more locations are in the ledger?" One of the younger monks asked, moving behind the leader to peer with sightless eyes at the book.

The leader flipped to the back section of the tome, the blank ledger, and began moving his finger down it, scanning.

"Oak Island is almost fully excavated, that location is no longer viable." He shook his head, using his thumb to wipe a small section of the ledger, erasing the invisible text from the book.

One of the younger monks spoke up, gazing at the ark all the while. "Has the cave in Mount Nebo been eliminated from the possibilities yet?" The remaining pages of the ledger were starting to run thin. Their last home, the burial chamber of Miriam, had lasted less than a century before being discovered.

"We could try the cave beneath the Basilica of Moses on Mount Nebo. The ark hasn't been in that basilica since Jeremiah put it there himself. I am fairly certain that the cave still remains hidden." Most of the monks nodded, pleased with the idea of hiding their prized relic in the cave.

"I know of a better place," one of the youngest monks said, stroking his long white beard in contemplation. "You know of the ancient city of Susia, right?"

"The city captured by Alexander and then sacked by Genghis Khan? Yes, we know the place well. The ark has never rested there, according to the ledger. No viable locations are listed for that city. What do you have in mind?" The leader was intrigued. He had never considered Susia to be a viable option, deep in the territory of Islam.

"It is called Tus now," the monk continued. "The Muslims renamed it some time ago. There is a mosque there, the Haruniyeh Dome. A great Muslim theologian is sleeping for eternity underneath the dome, in a natural cave used as a burial chamber. We can keep our vigil in Al-Ghazali's tomb, undisturbed for millennia."

"Yes," the leader replied, nodding and smiling, "Persia would be the perfect place to keep it safe. We shall move at once." The old monk took his crooked finger and drew the word 'Susia' into the blank ledger before closing the book and placing it in a deep pocket inside his robe. The seven blind men began readying the ark for travel.

Acknowledgements
Special thanks to the physicist who edited, the marine biologist who helped with all the messy parts, and the dogs that sat on my lap while I typed.

Cover art by Will Olthouse
www.unsilentwill.com

Made in the USA
Lexington, KY
26 January 2013